PEACHY VILLAINS

SWEET PEACH BAKERY #5.

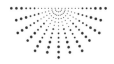

WENDY MEADOWS

MAJESTIC
OWL
PUBLISHING LLC

*T*he smell of hay, peanuts, popcorn, cotton candy and a little animal poo-poo filled Momma Peach's nose as she walked with Michelle through a maze of red and white striped tents toward the back of the large field. Her eyes wandered around each tent, spotting every kind of circus person there possibly was. A funny clown with a large red smile painted on his white- and blue-painted face walked past Momma Peach wearing a green and purple suit and a bright yellow wig. The clown glanced at Momma Peach, nodded, and hurried off. "My," Momma Peach whispered just as a large elephant walked around a tent and stopped directly in front of her. Momma Peach let out a shriek, grabbed Michelle's arm and ducked behind her.

"Oh now, really?" A pretty woman with dark red hair

asked in a strong Texan accent, "Melanie wouldn't hurt a fly."

Momma Peach peeked her head out from behind Michelle. Melanie the sweet elephant spotted Momma Peach, raised her trunk, and trumpeted a hello. Momma Peach winced in fear. "Hi...girl," she said and ducked her head back behind Michelle.

Michelle sighed. "Momma Peach, I think it's safe to come out."

"My name is Lidia Rye. And as I said, this here is Melanie."

"I'm Detective Chan and this is my partner, Caroline Johnson."

"Uh...call me Momma Peach," Momma Peach said and eased out from behind Michelle a second time. She looked at Melanie. The elephant looked at Momma Peach with a pair of innocent eyes. Momma Peach felt a strange warmth in her heart. Suddenly the horrifyingly big elephant no longer seemed terrifying. Instead, Momma Peach saw that the creature was gentle and caring. "Well, I'll be," Momma Peach smiled. "Why, hello, Melanie. I'm Momma Peach."

Melanie raised her trunk and let out a special greeting. Lidia smiled. "She likes you." Lidia patted Melanie's gray trunk. "Would you like to pet her?"

"Maybe later," Michelle said. "We're looking for Mr. Hayman."

Lidia stopped smiling and frowned. The woman, who wore a brown shirt and pants, had looked at ease, but the mention of Mr. Hayman's name made her stiff and uneasy. "He's in his trailer."

Michelle nodded. "Ms. Rye, did you know the man that was killed?"

Lidia sighed. "Yeah, I knew Lance. He was a good guy...one of the best, actually. I don't know why someone would want to kill that nice fella." Lidia shook her head. "Lance loved kids, you know. He was an amazing clown, always full of laughs and never had a hard word to say against anyone...although some folks around this circus deserve a hard word."

Momma Peach studied Lidia's pretty blue eyes. She liked Lidia. "Baby, can you—" Momma Peach was interrupted by an Asian woman with long black hair; the Asian woman appeared to be Michelle's age. But Momma Peach quickly saw the woman was Michelle's complete opposite. Michelle was a tough cop, but she had sweet, caring, brave eyes—the other woman had cold, mean eyes and a cruel face.

"Wasting time talking to the police?"

Lidia rolled her eyes. "Detective Chan, this is Lindsey Sung, Mr. Hayman's assistant."

Lindsey eyed Michelle with caution. Coincidentally, the two women were both dressed in black leather jackets and dark colored dresses. If Momma Peach didn't know better, she would have sworn the two were sisters. "Mr. Hayman already spoke to the police," she said in a hard voice.

"Not to me," Michelle fired back. "The murder scene is taped off. Forensics is wrapping things up. In the meantime, I need to speak to Mr. Hayman...right now."

Lindsey clearly didn't like taking orders from a cop— especially a female cop. "I said Mr. Hayman already gave his statement. If you want to speak to him, get a warrant."

"If Mr. Hayman refuses to speak to me I will consider him my number one suspect. I have cause enough to arrest him right here and now under suspicion of murder. Is that clear, Ms. Sung?" Michelle's voice told Momma Peach to stand back and get ready for a fireworks show to erupt. "I will also have the town pull Mr. Hayman's operational business license, too, and shut down this circus."

Lindsey balled her hands into two tight fists. *"You hide well behind a badge,"* she spoke in an insulting tone in Mandarin Chinese. *"Your kind are a disgrace to the old country."*

"Your kind is no better than sewer rats," Michelle said, switching to her own fluent Chinese language. Momma

4

Peach didn't know what Michelle said but whatever words left her mouth sure slapped her opponent in the face. "*I stand for light, you stand for darkness.*"

Lindsey Sung's dark eyes flashed with fury. She took two steps back and dropped down into a fighting position similar to the tense crouch Michelle always assumed before tangling with an enemy. "Let's see who ends up under the dirt," she hissed.

Michelle nodded and gently pushed Momma Peach behind her. "Stay back, Momma Peach," she warned.

"Now wait a minute, hold on," Lidia said, "let me get poor Melanie out the road before you girls go dragging." Lidia quickly walked Melanie out of harm's way.

Momma Peach wrapped her hand around her pocketbook. "She looks tough, Michelle."

Michelle stared into Lindsey's eyes. She didn't answer Momma Peach. Lindsey snarled in contempt and prepared to strike, but a firm voice threw cold water on her fire. "Settle down," a tall, thin man with a heavy British accent ordered Lindsey. "There is no need for any more violence in my circus."

Lindsey threw her head over her shoulder and spotted a handsome man in his mid-sixties walking up. He wore a finely pressed gray suit and carried a silver walking cane. She immediately stood down. She looked at Michelle. "Another time."

"Anytime," Michelle promised.

Momma Peach felt relief wash through her chest. Lindsey Sung scared her. "Are you Mr. Hayman?" she asked, hoping to quickly divert attention away from the fight that had been brewing.

Lionel Hayman raised his right hand and smoothed the thin, gray mustache over his lip. "I am he," he said.

Michelle examined the man's face. Lionel was not who she would have expected to find at a traveling circus. He reminded her of a stuffy English gentleman sitting in a peppermint pink parlor drinking tea and eating custard tarts. The round gray bowler covering his thin gray hair gave him a somewhat comical look, yet there was nothing comical about Lionel Hayman at all. "Mr. Hayman, I want to speak to you about Lance Potter."

"I've already spoken to a police officer and offered my full cooperation," Lionel replied and tapped the ground with his cane. "Ms. Sung, please find Mr. Ditton and have him clean the grounds. I will not tolerate such mess."

"Yes, Mr. Hayman," Lindsey responded in a sour voice. "He's probably drunk behind his trailer, as usual." Lindsey cast a threatening glare at Michelle as she walked away.

Lionel lifted his eyes and looked at Momma Peach. "Are you with the police force, madam?" he asked.

"I'm Momma Peach," Momma Peach said and stepped up to stand next to Michelle. "I work with Detective Chan when needed." Momma Peach didn't like the looks of Lionel. The stuffy man gave her the creeps.

Lionel simply nodded and focused on Michelle. "Detective Chan, as I mentioned, I have already spoken to a police officer. I am certain you can get everything you need from my statement. In the meantime, I do have a circus to manage."

"Mr. Hayman, I am the ranking detective on this police force and on this investigation, which means I have the final authority. You, sir, gave a statement to Officer Seth before I arrived." Michelle folded her arms. "I have certain questions that need to be asked and answered. You can either cooperate with me here or cooperate down at the police station. That is your choice."

Lionel gave Michelle a bored, annoyed face. "Of course," he stated. "You Americans are always so clumsy in your investigations, wasting valuable time irritating the innocent rather than pursuing the guilty." Lionel tapped the ground with his cane. "Very well, ask your questions, Detective."

"You don't seem upset about the death of one of your employees," Momma Peach pointed out.

"Why should I be?" Lance asked. "I barely knew the man. My assistant, Lindsey Sung, is in charge of scouting and hiring talent, and she also dismisses performers when needed. I did not know the deceased on a personal level because I prefer to maintain a professional relationship with all of the men and women employed at my circus."

Michelle glanced at Momma Peach. She could tell that Momma Peach wanted to smack Lionel in the head with her pocketbook. "Settle down, tiger," she whispered.

Momma Peach gritted her teeth. Lionel simply stared at her. "Is that all, madam?" he asked.

"No," Michelle continued. "Lance Potter was hired to perform as a clown, right?"

"Indeed. That is what my assistant informs me, and she checked his employment file." Lionel leaned forward on his cane.

"The man had no family...no wife...no children?"

"I had my assistant make a copy of Lance Potter's records and turn them over to the police officer I spoke with," Lionel explained. "If you ran a competent police force, Detective, you would know that already."

"No records have been turned over to my department," Michelle informed Lionel.

"I see," Lionel stated coldly and then glanced briefly in the direction Lindsey had walked off a few minutes before. "I must speak with my assistant, then. Perhaps she became distracted by another irritatingly persistent officer?" He looked back at Michelle, making his implication clear.

"Maybe," Michelle said. She looked to her right and saw three clowns staring at her from the doorway of a nearby tent. The clowns quickly slipped back into the tent and vanished. "I'm afraid I must repeat my question, Mr. Hayman. Did Mr. Potter have a wife or any children?"

"Mr. Potter's records state that he arrived for unemployment single, unattached. Whether the man had a wife or has any children elsewhere, I do not know. But as far as troublesome children or a woman traveling with him, I would think not. My assistant keeps a very tight leash on all of the men and women employed at my circus."

"Troublesome children?" Momma Peach asked. "Why, you overstuffed mushroom, this is a circus. Circuses are designed to bring happiness to children!" Momma Peach began to swing her pocketbook at Lionel. Michelle quickly pushed her arm down. "Oh, give me strength!" Momma Peach begged. "We're talking to a peanut head!"

"Madam," Lionel said in a calm voice, "my circus is simply a business. My goal is to turn a comfortable profit, not host a traveling daycare for my employees." Lionel tapped the ground with his cane to emphasize his words. "I offer simple, if adolescent, entertainment to the masses and in return, the masses yield to me the ticket price I demand for the show." He spread his hands and they could see a glimmer of the entertainer in him. "It is that simple. So, if you please, do away with your childish insults, madam. We are all adults...or so I assumed." He looked away as if bored by the conversation.

Momma Peach imagined her hands around Lionel's thin little neck. "Oh, give me strength, give me strength. I feel like I'm talking to a deranged man!"

Michelle fought back a grin. "Mr. Hayman, Lance Potter was found dead in his trailer early this morning by a man named Young Greenson." Michelle fought back a yawn as she glanced down to consult the scribbled words on her notepad. She was tired. "When I spoke to Mr. Greenson, he stated that he found Mr. Potter lying face-down on the floor with a knife stuck between his shoulder blades."

"Yes, my assistant told me," Lionel told Michelle and waved his left hand in the air as if he was swatting a pesky gnat away. "It appears that Mr. Potter acquired himself an enemy."

"Yes, it does," Michelle agreed. "Any idea who that enemy might be?"

"No," Lionel said, dismissing Michelle's question. "As I stated, Detective, I do not...mingle...with my workers. When you await a good meal, it does not do to trouble the servants who toil in the kitchen, if you will."

Michelle nodded. "Suits me just fine," she said to

Momma Peach. "There's better food in the kitchen because the food is cooked by honest hands, anyway."

Lionel frowned. "Are we quite finished?"

"Where were you this morning, Mr. Hayman?" Michelle asked in a stern voice. "I want time, location and, if possible, witnesses."

"Oh, very well," Lionel huffed. "I awoke at my usual time, which is five o'clock sharp. I ate a breakfast of beans, toast, and coffee and then began reviewing the payroll. My assistant joined me at eight sharp. At eight-thirty, Mr. Greenson arrived at my trailer in a panic and informed myself and my assistant about the untimely death of Mr. Potter. I, of course, immediately contacted the local police department." Lionel looked at Michelle with annoyance. "Now I have fully cooperated with the silly and unnecessarily rude investigation you Americans insist upon, and I must perform my usual inspections before tonight's show. As you know, the show must go on."

"Not tonight it won't," Michelle informed Lionel. "Mr. Hayman, a man was found dead. As of now, this circus is closed down and no one—and I mean not a single person —is to leave my town. Is that clear?"

Michelle's statement caused Lionel's cheeks to turn red. "You have no right to cancel—"

"I have every right and authority to do so," Michelle

interrupted Lionel. "You, sir, may continue your circus when and only when I give the green light to do so. In the meantime, I am going to fully investigate the death of one Mr. Lance Potter. As of now, sir, you are a suspect, along with everyone working for you. If you or any of your employees try to leave town, I will slap a warrant of arrest out on the wire so quickly it will make your heads spin. Do I make myself clear, sir?"

Lionel ground his cane into the dirt, leaving a deep divot out of barely suppressed outrage. "How long will you inconvenience me with your drabble?" he demanded. "I am a businessman, after all. Time is of great importance to me."

"When I find the killer, your circus will be back in business," Michelle informed Lionel. "In the meantime, I'm placing the fairgrounds under strict lockdown. This is a crime scene. No one comes or goes." Michelle stretched her neck. "I want you to gather every one of your employees, Mr. Hayman, and bring them into the main tent."

"Why?" Lionel demanded.

"I will interview every single person working for you," Michelle explained and looked at Momma Peach. "We're going to need lots of coffee, Momma Peach. And maybe some donuts?" she asked in a hopeful voice.

Momma Peach nodded. "Yes, lots and lots of coffee to

keep our eyes open today. A donut or two wouldn't hurt." Momma Peach looked at Lionel. The man sure gave her the creeps. "I'm going to help find out who killed the clown, rest his poor soul."

"In the great scheme of the world, madam, one dead clown is not a tragedy," Lionel stated and walked away into a gray, damp morning.

Young Greenson walked into the main tent through a side entrance used by the staff and maneuvered down an aisle between the metal bleachers that were stained with traces of sticky cotton candy and colorful sugar syrup from overpriced snow cones. The tent smelled of hay and animal dung mingled with wet grass and fear. In the middle of the tent was the center ring, protected by a wide wooden rail designed to separate the public from the performers. Inside the wooden circle there were no clowns, no elephants, no high wire, no trapeze, nothing except the damp grass and a very curious detective standing beside the woman named Momma Peach. Young was over-excited to speak to anyone, especially because Mr. Hayman was standing in the ring looking very annoyed and impatient. "Here we go," Young said and tested his breath to make sure he didn't smell like whiskey.

Michelle spotted Young testing his breath and could see

his glassy, bloodshot eyes from a distance. She nodded at Momma Peach and waited. Momma Peach studied every move Young made as he walked into the wooden circle. The man appeared to be in his late fifties, tall with a plump belly and short yellow hair that was messy as a wadded-up dishrag. She felt a sense of pity for the man. "Here I am, Mr. Hayman, right on time," Young said and glanced down at the gray button-down shirt he was wearing and quickly tucked it into his jeans. "Sorry about that," he said in a worried tone. Lionel shot him a look of displeasure.

"Oh, don't worry about not having your shirt tucked in," Momma Peach smiled at Young. "When I was a young wife, that used to be my favorite part about the morning, helping my handsome young man get dressed," she teased. "Speaking of, is there a Mrs. Greenson?"

Young glanced down at his worn sneakers and shook his head no. "I'm divorced, ma'am. My own fault...'m' drunk too much."

Lionel cleared his throat. "Detective Chan would like to ask you a series of questions, Mr. Greenson. I expect you to answer honestly if you expect to remain employed. Is that clear?"

"Yes, Mr. Hayman," Young said and nodded with a look in his eyes like a dog begging for approval.

Michelle folded her arms across her chest. It was clear to

her that Lionel Hayman held some form of authority over his employees that went beyond the usual boundaries of an employment arrangement. "Relax, Mr. Greenson. This is an informal inquiry. You're not in any kind of trouble. All I want to do is ask you a few questions, okay?"

Young slipped his hands into his pockets and nodded again. "Yes, ma'am."

"Please, call me Detective Chan."

"Yes, ma'am."

Momma Peach recognized Young's accent. The man was a Texan, like Lidia. "Relax," Momma Peach told Young. "Ain't no sense being tense."

"I reckon I should be tense," Young told Momma Peach in a worried voice. "Everyone around here knows Lance and me had issues with each other. I reckon I'm the number one suspect."

"Issues?" Michelle asked and looked at Lionel. Lionel was glaring at Young with cold eyes.

Young kept his eyes low. "Lance and I worked together as clowns. Only, we didn't work so well together. I reckon that was my fault because I...drank a lot and Lance, well, he worked through his time in the bottle and came out dry." Young shook his head. "Lance tried to help me kick the bottle, but I ended up turning him into my enemy."

"How's that?" Momma Peach asked.

Young glanced up at Lionel and then quickly returned his eyes to the ground. "It was a prank, really," he explained. "I got so sick and tired of Lance fussing at me to kick the bottle that...I slipped sweet liquor into his coffee before a performance." Young sighed. "He was a whiskey man, so he didn't recognize it at first...I told him it was one of them fancy flavored creamers and he drank it all up. Lance went out drunker than a skunk...oh, folks thought it was part of the act, and I didn't say a word...until now. Afterward, he figured it out. He stopped being my friend and turned sour toward me. I guess I had it coming."

"You do realize your confession just cost you your job," Lionel said coldly.

"I reckon," Young nodded miserably. "But Lance is dead, and he deserves a truthful mouth from this old drunk." Young looked up at Momma Peach, his head swaying a little on his neck. "Lance turned sour like I said, and we got into a few brawls...guess I was too stubborn to admit that I was the one in the wrong. I told him it was a joke, he told me I was an idiot and the drink would kill me one day if I didn't wise up. But I swear, I didn't kill him."

"Why did you go to his trailer this morning?" Momma Peach asked.

Young kicked at the damp ground. "Oh, last night Lance

and me tangled again, but not too bad. I slung him over a chair and he punched me in the stomach. The fight was my fault because he was sitting with Millie at supper again."

"Millie?" Michelle asked.

Young nodded. "Millie Frost. She handles the poodles," he explained. "She sure is a pretty woman and it's no secret Lance and me both want her hand in marriage...well, wanted her hand in marriage." Young ran his hands through his messy hair. "I felt pretty bad about the fight because, well...it upset Millie. Millie don't like violence and...well, dag-blast-it, the mess between Lance and me was all my doing. I needed to make it right, so I went to Lance's trailer this morning to make it right."

Momma Peach knew Young was speaking the truth. "You found Mr. Potter dead, rest his poor soul, right?"

Young nodded in sorrow. "Lance was lying face-down next to his couch...he had a knife...well, I already told you where he was stabbed." Young looked at Michelle. "I freaked out and ran to Mr. Hayman. I thought for sure folks would say I killed Lance, but I didn't. I swear it." Young looked down at his feet. "Millie is sure to hate me now," he whispered.

Michelle reached out and put a hand on Young's shoulder. "You need to sober up, Mr. Greenson, and take your life back from the shadows."

Young shook his head. "I already tried. The bottle is more powerful than me."

"Jesus is stronger than the bottle," Momma Peach promised Young and patted his shoulder. "It's never too late to get right with Jesus."

Young lifted his eyes and looked into Momma Peach's loving face. "I'm too old and worn-out to be of any good anymore. And now I'm an unemployed clown...a real loser."

"No," Momma Peach promised Young. "You're only a loser if you let yourself be."

"Oh, for goodness sake," Lionel complained. "Is this a police investigation or an AA intervention?"

Michelle shot Lionel a cold eye. "Mr. Hayman, I want to speak to Millie Frost."

"Oh, very well," Lionel said and pointed a hand at Young. "Go find your...friend, Mr. Greenson, and bring her to me and then begin packing your bags."

"Yes, sir," Young said and quickly walked away on stumbling feet.

Momma Peach looked at Lionel. "The man admitted his mistake. You should consider giving him a second chance."

"I don't give drunks second chances," Lionel scolded Momma Peach. "I run a business. Not a rehab facility."

Momma Peach wrapped her hand around the strap of her pocketbook and prayed for strength as she muttered to Michelle, "Michelle, station yourself between that dog and me because I am about to be on him like white on rice. Oh, give me strength, give me strength."

Lionel tapped the ground with his cane and looked away from Momma Peach and waited for Millie Frost to appear. While he waited, Michelle made a few notes in her notebook while Momma Peach composed herself. Momma Peach took a deep breath and studied the cane marks on the ground with skillful eyes. Twenty minutes later, a tall, pretty woman with black hair streaked with gray walked into the center ring. "You took long enough, Ms. Frost," Lionel said tersely.

"Oh, keep your shirt on," Millie fussed in a strong Texan accent. The woman had a pretty face and her eyes were full of fire and sass. "I got here, didn't I?" she asked and slowly tucked a blue shirt into her long, old West-style gray skirt. "I was washing my dogs for goodness sake. I can't just come running whenever someone bellows for me."

"Mind your manners," Lionel warned Millie. "Might I remind you that I am your boss?"

"Might I remind you that I couldn't care a dog's fart less?" Millie told Lionel. "Might I also remind you that I work this circus because I choose to, not because I have to. The interest I draw off of my money in one month is more than you pay me in a year. So shove it, pal. In fact...you know what? I quit. I'm not sticking around this dungeon any longer. I only stuck around this long because of Lance. And now that he's been killed, well, I'm making tracks back to Texas."

Momma Peach was impressed. She saw Michelle grin. Before Lionel could answer, Momma Peach jumped in. "Ms. Frost, as much as I would love to stand here and watch you tell this stuffy rat off, we do need to ask you some questions."

Millie turned her attention to Michelle and Momma Peach. "You want to know if I killed Lance, right?"

"Oh, I am sure you didn't kill anything but some pesky fleas," Momma Peach smiled. "What I want to know is, who was Lance Potter? Was the poor soul ever married? Did he have children?"

Lionel huffed at Millie. His power over her was lost. "Answer honestly, Ms. Frost."

Millie threw her hand at Lionel. "Oh, shut up you overgrown crumpet," she fussed and returned her attention back to Momma Peach. "Lance never had a wife or kids, I'm afraid."

"What's the man's story?" Michelle asked in a polite voice. "Any information would help, Ms. Frost."

"Oh, call me Millie," she told Michelle. "Ain't no reason to be calling me anything except my name."

"Okay then...Millie," Michelle smiled. "Millie, what do you know about Lance Potter?"

"Lance Potter was a sixty-one-year-old recovering alcoholic who never escaped his time in the Vietnam War," Millie began, her eyes wistful and sad. "After the war, Lance tried to go back to school, get a job, manage his life...but he ended up on the bottle and eventually he ended up homeless and living in an alley." Millie shook her head with sadness. "A preacher man found Lance and helped him turn his life around. But," Millie sighed, "Lance had to spend over a year in a mental hospital fighting a really bad depression."

"The poor soul," Momma Peach said.

"Eventually, Lance got his mind worked out and decided he wanted to become a therapist and work in a hospital where he could help sick children. That's what he did until he was fifty-four. But the sight of sick children finally took its toll on Lance, so he decided to join the circus and perform for all kinds of children." Millie focused on Michelle. "You gettin' this down, honey?"

"You bet."

"Lance joined the Spectacular Circus first and worked for Mr. Ridge for five years touring around Texas and Louisiana, Mississippi and Arkansas, all through that area. But when the Spectacular Circus went bankrupt, Lance found work at this dive. We both did."

"Both?" Michelle asked.

"Yeah," Millie explained. "I came to work for Mr. Ridge about two years after Lance did. After my husband died, you see. I couldn't see myself sitting around Texas feeling sorry for myself and, well, as silly as this may sound, ever since I was a little girl the circus has always fascinated me." Millie smiled. "When the Spectacular Circus came to Dallas, I decided to see a show. That's how I met Lance. It was Lance who convinced me to join the circus. But what did I know about a circus?" Millie nearly laughed and then almost began crying. "Lance suggested I learn how to train poodles. I thought he was crazy. But you know what?"

"What?" Momma Peach asked.

"I did learn, too," Millie wiped at a tear. "I'm sixty years old, ladies, and I've lived a full life. Now it's time for a new adventure, somewhere."

Momma Peach walked up to Millie and put her warm, loving arms around her. "You're a special woman, I can tell."

Lionel cleared his throat uncomfortably. "Can we focus on the questions at hand?"

Millie hugged Momma Peach and threw a sour look at Lionel. "Oh, keep your shirt on."

"Millie," Michelle asked, "Young Greenson confessed that he and Mr. Potter had their share of fights. Did Mr. Potter have problems with anyone else?"

"No," Millie said, "just Young. After Young put that liquor in his coffee last year, well, a man can only be pushed so far." Millie shook her head. "It wasn't that Lance was mad at Young for spiking his coffee, he was mad at Young because it was an insult to the children. The children, you see, were Lance's world and Young caused him to perform drunk in front of them. For a former alcoholic, it was his worst nightmare. Can you ladies understand that?"

"We sure can," Momma Peach promised.

"Yeah," Michelle sighed, "we sure can." Michelle looked around the empty ring. In her mind, she saw a bunch of clowns riding in tiny cars, honking horns, waving at smiling children. "Mr. Greenson seems to be letting his guilt eat him alive."

"Oh, Young isn't a bad guy," Millie pointed out. "It's no secret that he loves me, but I don't love him, not in the way a woman should."

"You loved Lance, didn't you?" Momma Peach asked.

"Oh, sure I did, but not romantically. Lance was a very special fella, but we never clicked romantically." Millie clasped her hands together. "Folks around here, especially Young, always said Lance was after my hand. The truth is, Lance was devoted to the children...he was married to their laughter, their smiles. The man would have made a great husband for a very special woman, but God has his reasons and Lance's purpose in life was to make children laugh. Lance and I were friends, same as Young and I, but I always held a special affection for Lance."

"Millie," Michelle asked, "the way you describe Mr. Potter makes him sound like a very likable person. But someone killed him. Are you sure Mr. Potter didn't have any other enemies, other than Mr. Greenson?"

"Not a soul that I can think of," Millie confessed. "Lance was well-liked by everybody, except his ongoing fight with Young, of course...and Ms. Sung. But Ms. Sung doesn't like anybody."

Momma Peach heard a gentle rain start falling outside of the tent and then felt her tummy rumble. "Well," she told Michelle, "let's take lunch and come back. I need to eat." Momma Peach looked at Millie. "Millie, do you want to join me for lunch?"

"Sure, why not," Millie said with a sad smile.

"I thought," Lionel said and cleared his voice, "my circus was under lockdown."

"Millie Frost is free to leave," Michelle informed Lionel. "We'll be back after lunch and continue with the questioning. In the meantime, stay on the fairgrounds, Mr. Hayman." Michelle looked at Millie. "Do you need to get your purse?"

"Nope," Millie said and patted her waist, "I carry my dough right here where no one can get to it." Millie looked at Lionel. "You know what, Lionel? I warned Lance it was time to leave but he insisted you had some good in you. He was wrong." And with those words, Millie walked away.

CHAPTER TWO

*M*omma Peach plopped down in a red and white booth and carefully eyed Mrs. Edward, the old woman who owned the diner, who sat at the front register just as pleasant as a bushel full of fresh peaches. "Oh, I just know she's going to serve some of those day-old biscuits again," Momma Peach groused to Michelle. "I must be starving if I'm willing to eat that woman's cooking."

Michelle sat down next to Millie, grinned at Momma Peach's usual protests, and then casually picked up a menu. The lunchtime crowd had passed, leaving the diner mostly empty except for a few senior citizens sitting around, drinking coffee and talking about the old days. Michelle couldn't blame the old-timers for making the diner their choice spot. The atmosphere in the diner was pleasantly old-fashioned and always smelled of coffee and delicious foods; of course, she would never tell Momma Peach that, goodness no—that would start a war. "We'll just have to pump our stomachs afterward, Momma Peach," Michelle said and zoomed in on a scrumptious chicken and dumplings plate.

Millie wasn't certain why Momma Peach chose to eat at the diner if she despised the cooking. "Would you like to eat someplace else?" she asked hesitantly.

Michelle let out a slight giggle. "Oh no, we're fine. You see," Michelle lowered her menu, "Momma Peach and Mrs. Edwards, the woman who owns this diner, have been at war with each other for quite some time."

"Oh, I see," Millie said. She spotted Mrs. Edwards placing a careful eye on Momma Peach. "Oh, I do see," she grinned. "Well then," she said and picked up a menu, "I guess I better choose me a meal...if I can get it down, of course."

"If you can eat that woman's food you'll be my hero," Momma Peach promised Millie and snatched up a menu. "Let's see...burnt meatloaf...soupy dumplings...greasy hamburger steaks..." Momma Peach mumbled to herself.

Michelle winked at Millie. Millie nodded. Even though she barely knew Momma Peach, she could sense that the woman's heart was very special, and her spirit was as soothing as a balm. "I think I'll have...oh, the chicken and dumplings plate," she said and placed her menu back down onto the table. "And maybe a glass of iced tea."

"Horridly sugary tea," Momma Peach mumbled under her breath. "It's so sweet you could stand a spoon upright in it. Mrs. Edwards is fixing to turn our poor bodies into mounds of melting fat at this rate."

"Perhaps coffee would be better," Millie quickly changed her mind. Momma Peach nodded in approval.

A young woman wearing a brown and white dress walked up to the table with a lovely smile and greeted them in a pleasant voice. "Momma Peach, you must be here to fuss over Mrs. Edward's cooking yet again. I do declare, you are something else."

Momma Peach raised her eyes and looked up at Jessica Braveton disapprovingly, but Jessica was already shaking her head. "You keep the doctor on speed dial, I might need a stomach pump after I eat that woman's food." Momma Peach tossed a thumb at Mrs. Edwards. Mrs. Edwards shook her head, raised her wooden cane, and shook it at Momma Peach. "Yeah, yeah, you old bat," Momma Peach griped, "you and your day-old biscuits will do me more harm than that cane of yours!"

Jessica rolled her eyes. "Those two," she said to Michelle. "What can I get you to drink? Coffee? Iced tea?"

"Coffee," Michelle told Jessica.

"Coffee, black," Millie said and looked up at Jessica. "My, the way you have your hair braided is lovely."

Jessica blushed. She touched her dark brown hair with her left hand. "My mother helped me braid my hair this morning."

Millie smiled. She never had children herself, but she had always considered every child in the world a part of her heart. Maybe that's why she and Lance got along so well, she always thought. "Well, you tell your mother she did a wonderful job."

"I'll have...oh, for goodness sake, bring me a cup of coffee...if you can get a spoon in it, that is. And you might as well bring me a burned meatloaf plate with some okra and mashed potatoes...some of them day-old biscuits and a slice of that awful apple pie."

"I heard that," Mrs. Edwards yelled at Momma Peach. "No senior discount for you!"

"Just pay my hospital bill after my meal, old woman," Momma Peach hollered back. "Gonna need an army of doctors to save my stomach after I eat your food."

Jessica rolled her eyes again. "Detective Chan?"

"I'll have the chicken and dumpling plate with okra and green beans," Michelle placed her order.

"Ma'am?" Jessica asked Millie.

"Oh, call me Millie, darling," Millie smiled. "I ain't an old woman yet." Millie watched Momma Peach fuss with the menu some more. "I think I'll have the chicken and dumpling plate too, with some okra and a sweet potato."

Jessica wrote down the orders, shook her head at Momma Peach, and walked back to the kitchen. "Momma Peach," Michelle said in an amused voice, "really?"

"Don't start in on me," Momma Peach warned Michelle. She dug in her purse for a peppermint. "I am in the war zone here, oh, give me strength, give me strength."

Millie couldn't help but smile. Her close friend was newly dead, but she found comfort in Momma Peach's silly theatrics. "So," she said, "how long has this war been going on?"

"For years," Michelle explained. Momma Peach pretended not to listen, still digging in her purse. "But," Michelle added in an undertone, "Momma Peach and Mrs. Edwards are secretly fond of each other, even though they'll never admit it."

"No discount for you, either," Mrs. Edwards warned Michelle and shook her cane in the air.

Michelle giggled again. "You see?"

"I see," Millie smiled. She grew silent and studied the atmosphere of the diner. Even though she had visited countless towns dotted across the American landscape,

31

there was something very special about this little Georgia town. What that something was, Millie didn't know. What she did know was that while she loved Texas, she had no desire to return to Dallas. Her old life was over, and she needed a new adventure; and besides, she had a promise to fulfill.

Millie began to speak when the front door of the diner opened, and a handsome man walked in wearing a cowboy hat. She saw Momma Peach raise her hand and wave at the man. "Over here, Mr. Sam."

Sam spotted Momma Peach and Michelle sitting with a strange woman and walked over to the booth. He removed his hat, ran a quick hand through his hair, and looked down at Momma Peach. "I called the station. Officer Mintly said y'all were here at the diner." Sam eyed Millie with a friendly look, smiled politely, and then looked back at Momma Peach.

"Is anything the matter, Sam?" Momma Peach asked Sam.

"Oh no, just hungry and didn't want to eat alone," Sam smiled.

"Well, slide on in," Momma Peach said and moved over to make room for Sam.

Michelle saw that Sam checked to make sure his gray shirt was tucked nicely into his blue jeans before he sat down. Why did he check his shirt? That's something a high school kid did in order to make sure he looked nice and cool in front of his girl. Michelle noticed Sam's strange expression and gave Momma Peach a funny look. Momma Peach simply smiled. Meanwhile, Sam had turned politely to Millie. "My name is Sam. I'm close friends with Momma Peach and Michelle...well, family really."

"I'm Millie Frost," Millie told Sam and felt her heart rate increase as she looked into his handsome face.

"Millie works...worked for the circus," Michelle explained. "Her close friend, Lance Potter, was found dead earlier this morning."

"I'm sorry," Sam said in a sincere voice.

"So am I," Millie replied. "Lance was a good man." Millie looked down at her hands. Her mind shifted away from Sam to Lance. "Detective Chan—"

"Michelle."

Millie nodded. "I've been thinking about your question earlier...I never saw Lance tangle with anyone except Young Greenson. I never even saw him have an argument with Lindsey Sung. I just can't imagine who would want to kill him. What I do know is that Young Greenson sure didn't. Young has a temper when the whiskey gets into his system, but he isn't a killer."

"Millie, tell me about Lindsey Sung," Michelle asked.

"I don't know much about the woman," Millie confessed. "All I know is that Lindsey Sung does all the hiring, firing, managing, payroll, bookings, purchases, stuff like that. She's one cold fish." Millie kept her eyes on low. "I never really saw the woman except before performances when she made her usual rounds to make sure everyone was prepared for the big show."

"Baby," Momma Peach asked, "have your eyes ever seen any funny business happening at that circus?"

Sam crossed his arms over his chest. He studied Millie's pretty face. The woman was upset but determined to be helpful. "No, not that I can recall. Circus life is a strange life, Momma Peach. One day you're in one town and the next you're in another town. People come and go like the wind, drifting in and out. But there's always the regulars who are always around, and it's those people you get to know."

"Keep talking."

Millie shifted in her seat. "I own a drivable RV, Momma Peach. Nothing fancy, but cozy and comfortable. That RV is my home. I call it my trailer because I like to use circus talk," Millie shook her head. "It's strange, but I really wanted to fit in with the circus life. I always enjoyed having some of the regulars over for coffee and Uno after a performance. We'd sit around, laugh, talk and throw insults around." Millie looked up at Momma Peach and smiled. "Those times were nice."

"And Lance was he always part of the family that came over to play Uno and have coffee?" Momma Peach asked.

Millie nodded. "Lance was always the first to arrive and the last to leave. He made the best coffee, too." Millie looked down at her hands again. "It's like I mentioned, there was no romance between us...but we did share a special bond."

Momma Peach looked into Millie's eyes and patted Sam's hand. "I understand."

Sam patted Momma Peach's hand back. "Momma Peach and I share a deep bond," he told Millie and then nodded at Michelle. "I think of Michelle as my own daughter, too."

Michelle blushed. She sure loved Sam and knew Sam loved her. "Millie, did Young Greenson ever join in on the card games?"

"Oh, sometimes, even though Lance never approved. He didn't like Young coming over drunk. None of us in my trailer ever drank, you see. But I..." Millie shook her head. "I always tried to make those two patch things up, but it was no use. Lance never got past Young spiking his coffee, and he sure never offered his hand in friendship again. And Young didn't exactly make it easy for Lance if he had wanted to offer him friendship again, either."

Momma Peach saw Jessica walking up to the booth. "Hello Sam, what can I get you today?" she asked.

"Well," Sam said hungrily and then caught Momma Peach giving him a warning eye, "I think...I mean, if my stomach can handle it...I'll have some of Mrs. Edwards' chicken and dumplings, a sweet potato and some okra...and coffee, black."

"You got it," Jessica smiled and walked away.

"Seems like you two have the same taste buds," Michelle pointed out. "Millie ordered the same meal you just did, Sam."

Millie looked up at Sam. She allowed herself to smile. "Do you like the circus, Sam?" she asked.

Sam made a thoughtful face, folded his arms again, and then shook his head. "I can't say...I've never been to a circus show before."

"Oh, how sad," Millie said in a tragic voice. "The circus...the right kind of circus...is filled with wonder, excitement, mystery and even a little danger. The circus is grand and adventurous." Millie's eyes became dreamy but quickly cleared up. "My time with the circus is over, though. That chapter of my life is now complete and I'm ready to begin a new chapter."

Sam wanted to tell Millie about his small desert town and how he, too, had to begin a new chapter in his own life. But he kept quiet instead. Momma Peach sure didn't. "Mr. Sam changed up his life not too long ago. He used to own this small town way out in the Nevada desert,"

Momma Peach said in a quick voice to let Sam know that she wanted to stir a little love in the air.

"Oh?" Millie asked.

Sam shot a wary eye at Momma Peach. "Yeah," he said and looked at Michelle for help. Michelle simply smiled. "I was never much on big city life," he explained. "My town is gone now, however."

Momma Peach heard sadness creep into Sam's voice. "Be that as it may," she added in a positive tone, "Mr. Sam may have lost his town, but he gained a family and we gained him." Momma Peach nudged Sam with her shoulder. "Mr. Sam is a real gold nugget."

Millie could tell that Momma Peach loved Sam and that Sam loved her. Their bond was unique and special. "How did you lose your town?" Millie asked.

Sam bit down on his lower lip. What was the harm in telling a strange woman his story, he thought. So he slowly eased forward into the tale of the day Momma Peach and Michelle arrived in his town and how from there, his life was changed forever. Millie listened to every word Sam spoke, barely noticing when Jessica brought out the drinks and food. She ate slowly, nodded her head at certain times, and studied Sam's eyes as he talked. By the time Sam finished his story, she sat utterly amazed. "Your own wife turned against you. How sad," she said and took the last sip of her coffee.

Sam mopped up the last of his chicken and dumplings with a biscuit and tossed the food into his mouth. As much as he still hurt inside, he refused to let the past cripple him. "In time, when a good friend in Alaska is ready, I'm going to buy his lodge. I guess that will become my new little town," Sam forced a smile to his face. "I have no desire to focus on my past...my dead wife...her hate...my lost town...ain't no sense in letting those things fuss with my mind anymore."

Millie admired Sam for his courage to rebuild a broken life. "My husband of twenty years died in a plane accident. He was flying his private plane from Dallas to Tucson when the engine failed." Millie slowly pulled her hands into her lap and looked down, reminiscing. "My Jason was full of life and heart. The world lost a good man." Millie looked at Michelle, then to Momma Peach and Sam. "In my husband's will, he asked me to live out my dreams as a special gift to him. It broke my heart a little that he had no idea he'd be making that request after such an untimely death, but I made a special promise that I would do just that...as tough as it is sometimes. Seems like you and I have something in common, Sam. We're both trying to recapture our dreams."

Sam stared at Millie and then slowly nodded. "I guess you're right."

"Well," Michelle said and stood up, "we better get back to

the fairgrounds. I'm sure Mr. Hayman is fuming by now. Sam, will we see you tonight for dinner?"

"Sure, y'all come over to the farmhouse. I'll whip us up a good meal. Millie, you should come, too," Sam said in a hopeful voice.

"We'll bring Millie," Momma Peach promised. "But we might be a tad late for supper," she explained. "I know there's foul play going on at that there circus, and we're going to get to the bottom of the rotten barrel if it takes all afternoon."

Momma Peach stood up, hugged Mr. Sam, and walked up to the front register and prepared to battle Mrs. Edwards over the bill and the allegedly terrible food. Sam, Michelle, and Millie stood back and watched the war begin. By the time the dust cleared, Momma Peach had managed to win a two percent discount off her apple pie because a bit of the crust had come out a tad burnt, and Momma Peach had triumphantly produced the proof, wrapped up in a napkin.

When Momma Peach and Michelle returned to the fairgrounds with Millie and walked into the main tent, they spotted Lindsey Sung standing beside Lionel. Lindsey cast an angry glare at Michelle. "I have contacted Mr. Hayman's attorney. He has instructed Mr.

Hayman to remain silent until he arrives from Los Angeles tomorrow afternoon." Lindsey nearly gritted her teeth to dust as she spoke. "We were hoping this matter could be settled without the involvement of Mr. Hayman's attorney, but since you're insisting on complicating the matter, you may expect legal intercession on his behalf."

Lindsey's words didn't bother Michelle. "If Mr. Hayman has nothing to hide, we won't have a problem," she told the other woman, not bothered one hair by the idle threats. "Now, I would like to continue with the questioning."

"Mr. Hayman has advised all of his employees to remain silent and speak to legal counsel only," Lindsey fired at Michelle. "So unless you have a warrant, I suggest you leave the premises."

"This is county land," Michelle informed Lindsey with a daring stare, "and I'm a law enforcement officer conducting an investigation into the murder of an innocent man. Right now, this circus is under lockdown and no one is going anywhere. You can hire all the legal counsel you want, but we have our own team of attorneys who don't back down from a fight." Michelle looked at Lionel. "If you are innocent, sir, then it would seem that you would be willing to cooperate with the law instead of setting up unnecessary hurdles."

Momma Peach studied Lionel's eyes. The snake was

hiding something and using his hired ninja, or whatever Lindsey was, to speak for him. The situation had changed while she was away fussing with Mrs. Edwards over the food.

Lindsey turned as if to leave and said, "Unless Mr. Hayman is being placed under arrest—"

"If Mr. Hayman, or anyone else for that matter, leaves this fairground, they will be placed under immediate arrest," Michelle warned Lindsey. "And since Mr. Hayman's employees have been ordered not to speak to the police except through his legal counsel, it looks like I'm going to have to book everyone as a clear suspect, which means I will be automatically granted warrants to search their personal trailers." Michelle tossed a thumb at a large cop standing at the entrance to the main tent. "I have my men patrolling the fairgrounds. If they see any funny business, they'll begin making arrests."

"There's a tall fence running around this here field," Momma Peach added. "I wouldn't try to jump that fence, either. You'd be smart to cooperate instead of playing the part of the stubborn donkey because I am going to find out who killed poor Mr. Potter, rest his soul."

"I'm going to pull my RV out of this gray cloud," Millie told Michelle and began walking away. Lindsey followed her with snake-like eyes.

"The autopsy report on Mr. Potter will be on my desk by

tomorrow," Michelle told Lionel. "I'll be back when your attorney arrives. In the meantime, I'm going to examine the grounds and look around."

"You have no legal—"

"I have every legal right," Michelle snapped at Lindsey. "As it stands, until I get the warrants I need, I can only search the public grounds and not personal trailers or belongings. It would be smart to cooperate with me instead of throwing suspicion into your corner."

"I'll have your badge," Lindsey threatened Michelle. "Your brutal intimidation tactics against Mr. Hayman will be condemned in your pathetic American courts. The British Embassy will hear of this, too."

"Don't give me that garbage," Momma Peach fired at Lindsey. "Listen you low-down, good for nothing, yellow-belly, miserable excuse for a human being, don't you dare stand there and make that man out to be the victim when a good man has been killed. Oh, give me strength to deal with these two vermin!" Momma Peach yelled.

Lindsey snarled at Momma Peach, her lip curling in disgust. "Mr. Hayman is a legitimate businessman currently suffering a great deal of stress and doesn't deserve your foolish hostility. If your harassment against him continues, we will be forced to bring lethal legal action against the police department of this miserable little town. If you cease your ugly actions, we will agree to dismantle the circus and locate to a new location."

"If you leave, I'll get to you," Michelle warned Lindsey.

"And I will be right on your backside like white on rice," Momma Peach promised.

"This circus remains under lockdown until I give the green light, is that clear?" Michelle fired at Lindsey.

"Don't cross me," Lindsey warned Michelle. "Do as I say and save your job...and your life."

"You're a disgrace," Michelle told Lindsey and patted her badge, which was hooked to the martial arts black belt around her waist. "Honor takes courage."

"Cowards die behind a badge," Lindsey hissed at Michelle. She then turned and focused on Lionel. "Would you like to return to your trailer?" Lionel nodded, tapped the ground with his cane, and walked away with Lindsey at his side.

"Seems like while we were eating," Momma Peach said, watching Lionel and Lindsey leave the tent through a side entrance, "those two snakes created a new hole to hide in."

"Yeah, seems that way, Momma Peach," Michelle agreed. "Come on, let's take a walk around."

Michelle took Momma Peach's arm and they walked to

the back of the tent and outside. She paused and studied the sea of vehicles hooked to run-down trailers, red and white tents, cages full of animals, vending carts, and various carnival games—but what she didn't see were people. "Folks seem to have vanished," Momma Peach said. "Creepy, isn't it?"

Michelle nodded. "Mr. Hayman has some kind of power over some of these people, Momma Peach."

"Job security," Momma Peach explained and spotted Melanie the elephant standing in a large metal cage. "Oh, how sad," she said and hurried over to the cage. Lidia appeared. "Oh, hey...oh, what's the matter?"

Michelle spotted a worried, grieved expression on Lidia's face. "I've been fired," Lidia explained and gave Melanie a sad look. "Lindsey Sung gave me my last paycheck about half an hour ago."

"Why were you fired?" Momma Peach asked.

"I think Mr. Hayman is having Lindsey Sung fire anyone that he thinks isn't loyal to him," Lidia explained. She looked at Michelle. "Detective Chan, I know you locked the circus down, but I can't stand to stay here any longer and see my girl locked in this awful cage."

Momma Peach understood Lidia's pain, but she also knew that if they let Lidia leave, Mr. Hayman's attorney would have a field day. Allowing Millie to leave was going to cause a whole lot of problems, too.

"Baby, you better stick around." Momma Peach looked at Michelle.

"I was thinking the same thing," Michelle sighed. She patted Lidia on her shoulder. "Everything will be okay," she promised.

"How?" Lidia asked. "Melanie is my girl. I can't imagine my life without her. If...if I had the money to buy her, I would. But that means I would need land to house her, a permit, the works. I barely have enough cash to buy myself food." Lidia patted the metal bars of the cage. Melanie stuck her trunk out and hugged Melanie's hand. Momma Peach nearly began crying.

"Leave everything up to me," she promised Lidia and wiped a tear away from her eye. "I am not going to let you and Melanie lose each other." Momma Peach grabbed Michelle's hand and walked her toward Lance Potter's trailer.

Officer John Downing was standing guard in front of the trailer, his tall, thin figure slumped a little in boredom. "Hey, John," Michelle said. "See anything peculiar while we were gone?"

John scratched his long nose. "Saw that cute Asian girl making some rounds, talking to some people, and then walk into the main tent with that Hayman fella." John shrugged his shoulders. "Been real quiet ever since."

Momma Peach looked past John and studied a red and

green striped trailer hooked to the back of a rundown gray Chevy Suburban. Yellow police tape was wrapped around the trailer. Inside the trailer sat the belongings of a decent man who had been murdered. It hurt her heart to see it. "Just plain awful," she whispered.

"John, Millie Frost has been given permission to leave the grounds. Go to her RV and make sure she leaves safely, okay?" Michelle ordered John. "She's over there." Michelle pointed to her right. In the distance, Millie could be seen packing a few lawn chairs into a bright yellow and brown RV. John nodded and strolled away. "Ready to go inside?" Michelle asked Momma Peach.

"I wasn't ready the first time," Momma Peach replied. "It's never easy going into a man's home and rummaging through his personal life after he's passed from God's earth." Momma Peach stared at the trailer. She looked down at the ground, preparing herself mentally to walk forward and cross the threshold of the trailer. Then she looked a little closer at the muddy ground. "Well I'll be, these weren't here earlier," she told Michelle and pointed down at the ground with her left hand while holding her pocketbook out of the way.

Michelle bent down and ran her hand lightly over the damp ground. "Cane marks," she said.

Momma Peach nodded. "Mr. Hayman has been here," she said. Momma Peach lifted her head and saw Officer

Downing talking to Millie. "Hey, bub," she yelled and waved her hand in the air, "get your tail back over here."

Officer Downing made a confused face and jogged back to Lance Potter's trailer. "What is it, Detective?" he asked.

Michelle glanced up at Officer Downing and read his face. "You left your station."

"Huh?" Officer Downing asked. He began shaking his head no. "No way, Detective. I'm been standing guard for hours."

"Don't lie, boy," Momma Peach warned Officer Downing. "See those little holes in the grass?"

Officer Downing looked down at the ground. He spotted a few tiny holes in the ground near the front door of the trailer. "Yeah, so?"

"Those marks were made by Mr. Hayman's cane," Momma Peach stated. "Those marks weren't here when me and Michelle were here earlier."

"Why did you leave your station, Downing?" Michelle asked in a patient, professional tone. She stood up. "I want an honest answer."

Officer Downing knew he was in trouble and fighting for a lie sure wasn't going to save him. "Okay, okay," he said and raised his hands into the air, "I did leave my station."

"Why?" Momma Peach asked, holding back her tongue.

"That cute Asian girl...she asked me to go with her while she canned some lady...the elephant lady," Officer Downing explained in a nervous voice. "She was worried the woman she was going to fire might cause trouble. I wasn't gone from my station...maybe ten minutes at the most."

"You were given strict orders to remain on guard at this location," Michelle said and shook her head in disappointment. "You're on desk duty for a month, Officer Downing. Go radio Officer Catoosa to take your place and get back to the station and start pulling front desk duty until I get back."

"Yes, Detective," Officer Downing said and hurried away in shame.

"So that snake slithered into Mr. Potter's trailer unseen," Momma Peach said in an angry voice. "No wonder his tone has changed." She looked at Officer Downing jogging away. "I might have been too hard on him. We all make mistakes. Go easy on him."

"Downing is a good guy. He has low self-esteem, though. I'll bet anything Miss Sung saw that too and knew she could use it to her advantage. Well, I'll make him write reports for a month and send him back out on duty. This is the first time he's sidestepped off the path, so there's really no sense in writing him up. She knew her pretty smile could be used as a weapon," Michelle explained.

"Speaking of that pretty smile, here she comes, the snake," Momma Peach said as Lindsey Sung walked toward the trailer.

"What is it, Sung?" Michelle asked.

Lindsey stopped a few feet away from Michelle. "Listen, cop," she said in an annoyed voice. "I'm giving you fair warning to back off, or else. You're in way over your head."

"You're not willing to teach me how to swim, are you?" Michelle asked lightly.

Lindsey eyed Momma Peach. "Back off or else," she warned again. "You know the old ways, cop. You're not just fighting me, and you know that."

"There's an easy way to get rid of me. Just tell me the truth. Who killed Lance Potter?" Michelle demanded.

Lindsey stared at Michelle. It was clear that the bold officer was a fighter and wasn't going to back down. "You're acting very reckless," she told Michelle and pointed a hard finger at her. "This is my last warning. Heed my warning for your own benefit and we can forget about our little fallout."

"Who killed Lance Potter?" Michelle demanded again. "I

want answers, Sung. If you refuse to answer my questions, I'll find someone who will."

Lindsey shook her head in disgust. "You've been warned," she said and looked at Momma Peach. "You would be smart, lady, to run."

"I don't run from snakes," Momma Peach told Lindsey and gripped her pocketbook and swung it into the air. "I terminate snakes, oh yes sir and yes ma'am."

Lindsey backed away from Momma Peach. "You've been warned," she hissed and walked away.

Michelle felt like chasing after Lindsey and going toe-to-toe with the woman. Instead, she focused her mind on the trailer. "Come on, Momma Peach, let's see what's waiting for us inside."

Momma Peach stopped swinging her purse. "Give me strength, give me strength," she said and followed Michelle into the trailer and found an ugly surprise.

CHAPTER THREE

The inside of Lance Potter's trailer was cramped, cluttered with racks of clown costumes, boxes full of props, toys and candy, a single green couch that folded out into a bed, and a small kitchen area with a round table. The floor was covered with an old green linoleum that made Momma Peach think of the old days—the good days. But her attention was quickly brought back to the future when she spotted an ugly whiskey bottle sitting halfway under the couch. "Now Momma Peach knows that poison bottle wasn't here when we combed this poor man's trailer earlier," Momma Peach told Michelle.

Michelle pulled a pair of latex gloves out of her right jacket pocket, slid the gloves on, bent down, and retrieved the whiskey bottle. The bottle was empty except for maybe a tiny sip left in the bottom. "What do you want to bet that we're going to find Young Greenson's fingerprints all over this bottle and maybe even a matching saliva sample?" Michelle stood up and shook her head. "Momma Peach, Mr. Greenson has just been framed."

Momma Peach nodded. "And you have no choice but to run that bottle and check for prints and go after the person the prints belong to."

"I can't suppress evidence," Michelle said in a regretful voice, "even if I think the evidence was planted. I have to follow the false trail while I look for the real one. Right now, we have no way of proving Mr. Hayman planted this bottle here." Michelle looked around the trailer. She spotted a green and purple clown costume hanging at the back of the trailer. In her mind she saw a kind, decent, funny man singing to himself as he put on the costume, preparing to bring laughter to hundreds of smiling children. "So sad," she whispered.

Momma Peach nodded and forced her mind to remain focused. "Honey, what did that woman mean when she said you weren't just fighting her?"

Michelle turned around and looked at Momma Peach. "In the old country," she said in a steady but worried voice, "dangerous, powerful men would gather into one force and dominate a certain area. Their power would expand over time, allowing them to control the innocent." Michelle looked down at the bottle in her hand. "Think of it like the mafia, Momma Peach, but ten times more deadly. We're talking about men who run drugs, guns...people. Men who control not just the dark side of the law, but also shipping ports, entire cities, government power...the works," Michelle finished.

Momma Peach rubbed her chin with her left hand. "I think I understand. But what makes my mind wonder is one simple question."

"You're wondering what powerful men are doing connected to a small circus, right, Momma Peach?"

"Yes. How can a bunch of criminals get connected to this little circus?" Momma Peach answered Michelle. "Is that stuffy old English muffin and his bodyguard using the circus as a front to run drugs?"

Michelle shook her head. "I don't think so," she answered honestly. "If Sung belongs to the group of people I think she does, then they wouldn't risk putting dirt in the gears by using a small circus to transfer simple dirty goods. It's something more."

"Money?" Momma Peach asked.

Michelle shook her head no again. "No, Momma Peach, if this circus is being used as a secret operation, then more is at stake than just money." Michelle looked back at the green and purple clown costume. "Somehow, Mr. Potter found out the answer we're seeking and was killed."

Momma Peach nodded. "I love when you read my

thoughts." Momma Peach studied the trailer. "The poor soul must have overheard a conversation between Hayman and Sung...or seen something he shouldn't have." Momma Peach grew silent and then spoke with an anguished, angry voice: "Could that awful woman have killed poor Mr. Potter herself?"

"Sung is a hired killer," Michelle mused. "Her kind are easy to recognize. She's a woman without a soul who thrives on power, cruelty, control and money." Michelle studied the bottle in her hand and then stuffed the bottle into her jacket. "I guess I need to get this whiskey bottle down to the station, Momma Peach. I don't think we're going to find much more today with the boss man and his hired gun threatening them all to keep silent."

Momma Peach nodded. "For now, let's make our two snakes believe we've fallen into their hole." Momma Peach tapped the small table in the trailer with her left hand. "We both know Young Greenson didn't kill poor Mr. Potter, rest his soul, but," she said in a careful tone, "we need to make two deadly people believe we do."

"Then let's go speak to Mr. Greenson," Michelle said. Before she left the trailer, her heart soaked in the sad sight of empty clown costumes once more. "So sad," she repeated and walked outside.

"Sad indeed," Momma Peach whispered. She followed Michelle outside and closed the door to the trailer behind her. A heavy drizzle had begun to fall. Summer was quickly fading away. "What a gray day."

"It seems fitting," Michelle agreed, looking around at the quiet circus grounds. "Young Greenson's trailer is over there," she said and pointed to a rusted red trailer hooked to a rundown pick-up truck. Young Greenson was nowhere in sight. "Ready?"

"I have a heavy heart right now. But I'm determined to catch the bad guys. Let's go."

Momma Peach followed Michelle over the damp grass, looking around as she walked, wondering what unseen eyes were watching her every step. The atmosphere of the circus was silent and creepy, the gray rainclouds casting an eerie gloom over the fairgrounds. Somewhere, either hidden in the parked trailers or tents, lurked a deadly killer they had yet to find; that is, assuming the killer wasn't Lindsey Sung. Momma Peach wasn't so sure Lindsey Sung was the killer—not yet anyway.

As they approached Young Greenson's trailer, Momma Peach spotted an old man peeking at them around the corner of the large, striped tent. It was someone they hadn't seen before. For a moment, he looked as if he wanted to speak to them, but then fear crossed his features and he retreated into his shell. He disappeared. "In time," Momma Peach promised, "we'll talk."

Michelle stopped at the front door of Young Greenson's

trailer, glanced around, and then knocked. "Mr. Greenson, it's Detective Chan," she said in a loud voice. "I need to talk to you." Silence followed. "Mr. Greenson," Michelle said and knocked on the trailer door again, "this is Detective Chan, I need to talk to you." More silence. Michelle looked at Momma Peach, bent down, withdrew a gun from her ankle holster, and stood up. "Mr. Greenson?" she asked in a loud voice, "are you inside? Are you okay? Are you hurt?" Silence again. "I'm going in, Momma Peach."

"I'm right behind you." Momma Peach prepared her pocketbook for battle.

Michelle reached out, grabbed the door handle and twisted it, yanked the door open and stormed inside the trailer. "Mr. Greenson—" Michelle said and then stopped. Her words fell down onto an ugly brown carpet like heavy stones.

"What is it?" Momma Peach asked worriedly. She ran into the trailer and slid to a stop. "Oh my," she said in a tragic voice and quickly turned her face down to the floor.

Young Greenson was hanging by the neck from a rope in the middle of his trailer. A note was pinned to his shirt and a spilled bottle of whiskey lay under his feet. Michelle backed away and eased Momma Peach outside. "Are you okay, Momma Peach?" she asked.

Momma Peach didn't answer at first. Instead, she looked back at Lance Potter's trailer. "God rest that man's soul, but the planted whiskey bottle belongs to a dead man who can't speak the truth now..." she whispered. "I ain't gonna let two poor men die for nothing. I'm gonna catch me some really bad people."

Three hours later, Michelle walked Momma Peach into her office at the police station. Momma Peach sat down in front of Michelle's desk, placed her pocketbook in her lap, and stared at the desk phone. Michelle plopped down in her chair, fought back a yawn, and took a sip of strong coffee from a brown paper cup. "It's been a long day, Momma Peach."

"Yes, it has," Momma Peach agreed. "We still have to have supper with Mr. Sam. After supper I'm going to go home and sleep a good night's sleep." Momma Peach fought back a yawn of her own. She felt frustrated and angry. "That fake suicide note is going to be tough to get past," she told Michelle.

"I know," Michelle sighed. She grew silent and listened to a light rainfall outside. "The whiskey bottle, the suicide note...doesn't look good."

"Nope, it sure doesn't. And what's worse is that not a single employee at the circus will talk," Momma Peach said. She raised her eyes and looked at Michelle. "That old geezer I saw looking at me might talk, but I know he has to come to me on his own."

Michelle leaned back in her chair and placed her hands behind her head. "Maybe," she said. "We can hope. In the meantime, I have no ground to hold anyone on. We have a suicide note written by a man confessing he killed Lance Potter. Right now, the case is practically solved. Mr. Hayman's attorney will eat me alive if I try to hold the circus in town." Michelle closed her exhausted eyes. "We lost this battle, Momma Peach. The odds were stacked again us."

Momma Peach wanted to argue, but how could she? Michelle was right. The case was lost—for the time being. Momma Peach had a plan, but first, she needed sleep. Her mind felt foggy and tired. A skilled detective knew when to back off and rest before retaliating. "I'm not a cop."

Michelle removed her hands from behind her head, leaned forward, and gave Momma Peach a curious eye. "Momma Peach?"

Momma Peach reached down and retrieved a piece of peppermint candy from her purse. "I don't need a search warrant. I'm just nosy, you see," Momma Peach explained with a sly wink. She popped the peppermint candy into her mouth and nodded. "I want to take a look in Mr. Hayman's trailer. In order to do so, I'm going to need you to cause a major distraction."

"Too risky," Michelle objected.

"Oh, not with Old Joe at my side," Momma Peach grinned. "Old Joe can pick a lock quicker than you can fuss about your laundry having too much starch." Momma Peach chewed on her peppermint. "Lindsey Sung is a problem. I need you to make double sure that woman is preoccupied."

"But," Michelle began to argue but stopped. She began wondering what Momma Peach and Old Joe might find in Lionel's trailer. Surely, she thought, the man would have valuable papers locked in a safe or hidden someplace that only a skilled thief could locate. Old Joe was a skilled thief. "Can Old Joe pick a safe?" she asked Momma Peach in a quick, low voice, glancing at her office door to make sure it was closed tight.

Momma Peach nodded. "Old Joe may look like a used-up dishrag, but that man still has plenty of smarts in his brain...along with some rottenness that I'm beating out of him with my pocketbook. I'm sure Old Joe can help me find anything that might be important to the case." Momma Peach fought back a second yawn. "A snake planted a whiskey bottle in poor Mr. Potter's trailer to push us into a corner. I'm going to plant a trap to keep that snake in town."

Michelle considered Momma Peach's offer. "We do need time," she agreed. "Mr. Hayman will have his circus out of town by sundown tomorrow night if we don't stop him."

"I'm not going to let that man or his circus skip town without us getting the bad guy," Momma Peach promised Michelle. "Oh, give me strength," she yawned, "I thought the little bit of trouble we faced in Alaska was the end of our worries. That cozy lodge sure sounds good right about now."

"I know," Michelle agreed. "The bed in my room was super soft and really warm," she said in a nostalgic voice. "I remember Able and me taking our romantic walk down to the lake under the full moon, holding hands..." Michelle closed her eyes. She saw Able's dorky but loving face appear in her mind. "Oh, my clumsy little hero," she whispered lovingly.

Momma Peach smiled. She knew that someday Michelle and Able were going to get married. When? She really didn't know and the when didn't really matter. What mattered the most in her heart was that Michelle had finally found love with a man that was faithful, caring and brave, even if he was a little geeky and clumsy at times. "Why don't you call Able?"

Michelle shook her head no. "Able is helping Mitchel right now. And if I call him he'll hear the worry in my voice and take the first flight down. I don't want Able anywhere near Lindsey Sung, Momma Peach."

"I understand," Momma Peach promised. She stood up, walked over to the office window and opened the blinds. Night had fallen. A wet, strange fog was stalking the night like a wounded, angry predator searching for an innocent victim to devour. "Oh, stop it," Momma Peach begged her mind. "Ain't no sense in thinking like that, now is there? Must be them awful day-old biscuits that old woman forced me to eat today."

"Speaking of biscuits, I'm starved," Michelle admitted. She stood up and walked over to Momma Peach. "Millie should be parked in front of your bakery by now. Let's go pick her up and drive out to Sam's place, okay?"

"Okay," Momma Peach caved in. "You don't have to twist my arm. A nice dinner at Mr. Sam's farmhouse rings a lovely bell in my mind. Let's just hope that Mr. Sam doesn't soak everything he cooked in cayenne pepper. Oh, give me strength, I was set on fire last time we ate at Mr. Sam's farmhouse."

Michelle winced. "Yeah, me, too," she said in a worried voice. "You don't think...I mean...he wouldn't...not again, right, Momma Peach?"

Momma Peach sighed. "Mr. Sam loves his cayenne pepper. All we can do is wait and see if the fire department is going to be needed after supper."

Michelle winced again. "Maybe I should stay here at the station and work—"

"Oh, no you don't," Momma Peach yelled and grabbed Michelle's hand, "If I'm going to suffer tonight, you're going to suffer right along with me. Let's go."

Michelle winced for a third time and grabbed an extra bottle of water from her office before leaving.

Sam's old farmhouse sat off alone by itself down a cozy country back road. The farmhouse was worn but built to last. The floors were old and creaked, the ceiling leaked, and the doors stuck, but the house was still standing after eighty years. Sam took pride in the farmhouse and he was patiently making needed repairs to the house—and the old barn—when he had the time, and he still managed to keep the original style of the farmhouse. Of course, Momma Peach thought, walking into a small living room holding a used brown recliner Sam had found at a yard sale and the ugliest brown and green couch she had ever seen, a woman's touch never hurt matters any. "Mr. Sam, oh, that couch...my eyes," Momma Peach exclaimed and shook a little rainwater off her damp dress.

Sam looked at the couch. "You fuss about that couch every time you come over," he said and rolled his eyes. "I think it's a great couch."

"You would," Momma Peach continued to fuss. "Baby, you have money so explain to me why you bought your furniture at a yard sale?"

Sam waited until Michelle and Millie were in the living room before continuing. Millie looked beautiful in her blue dress. Sam guessed he looked halfway decent in his black button-up shirt tucked into his blue jeans. "I like furniture that has character," he explained and closed the front door. "The furniture you find in the stores today...pure junk," Sam finished.

Millie studied Sam's ugly couch. She had to admit the couch was an eyesore. The living room itself wasn't half bad—cozy, actually. She spotted an old stone fireplace where an inviting fire crackled warmly. The wood-paneled walls were made of quality wood and complimented the hardwood floor that creaked under her feet. Some new furniture, flowers, pictures...a little paint here and there...and she could turn the living room around in no time. "It's...nice," she said and caught Momma Peach staring at her. Momma Peach read her eyes and flashed a happy smile. Millie blushed.

Sam rubbed the back of his neck. "Yeah, I'm still working on the place," he explained.

Michelle drew in a deep breath of freshly baked pumpkin pie and hot coffee. Her stomach cried out for the kitchen. "Uh, Sam, what's for dinner?" she asked.

Sam continued to rub the back of his neck. "Well, I took a nap earlier and kinda overslept so I...well, I had to order takeout."

"From the diner?" Momma Peach asked through gritted teeth.

63

Sam quickly moved behind Michelle. "Now Momma Peach, I had no choice. I ordered us all a turkey and dressing plate, pumpkin pie and some bread. But the coffee you're smelling is my own, I promise."

Momma Peach glared at Sam. "You traitor!" she cried out in pain. "Oh, give me strength, Mr. Sam has betrayed me."

"Now Momma Peach," Sam begged. "I didn't mean to oversleep—"

"I bet you didn't," Momma Peach said and shook her head. "Well, let me go into the kitchen and examine the poison you're going to serve for supper." Momma Peach walked out of the living room and found her way into an old-fashioned kitchen that made her heart yearn for the old times. The kitchen reminded her of grandmothers cooking fresh apple pies while children played outside in warm fields. "The good old days," Momma Peach sighed and put her pocketbook down on a brown wooden counter next to a coffee pot holding fresh, delicious coffee. She turned and focused her attention on the square wooden table sitting in the far corner of the kitchen. On the table sat four take-out containers from Mrs. Edwards' diner, along with a bag of rolls. "I have spotted the poison," Momma Peach said and looked at the dark gray stove next to the kitchen sink. The oven was on low, keeping the pumpkin pie warmed and ready to eat. "Where's my stomach pump?"

Michelle walked into the kitchen, spotted the coffee pot, and made a straight line toward the kitchen counter. "Coffee," she said in a hungry voice, snatched open a wooden cabinet, fished around, and grabbed a green coffee mug. "Momma Peach, coffee?"

"Yes, please."

Michelle took down three more green coffee mugs and filled them full of coffee as Sam and Millie walked into the kitchen. "Ah, coffee," Millie said in a happy voice. "After the day I had, I could sure use a fresh cup of java."

Sam saw sadness enter Millie's eyes. "I heard about Mr. Greenson. I'm sorry," he told Millie.

Millie walked over to the kitchen table and sat down. She sat silently for a minute and explored the kitchen with tired but curious eyes. The kitchen sure needed a woman's touch. "I don't believe for one second Young killed himself," she finally spoke.

Sam took a mug of coffee from Michelle and walked it over to Millie. "Here's your coffee."

Millie took the coffee. "Thanks."

Sam smiled. "Anytime," he said and walked over to the kitchen counter and leaned against it. "So it seems that there's a double murder at play, right?" he asked.

Michelle handed Momma Peach her coffee. Momma

Peach took a careful sip. "Mr. Sam, I don't know how you do it, but you make the best coffee I have ever tasted."

Sam smiled. "Years of experience, Momma Peach, years of experience."

Michelle didn't smile. She walked over to the kitchen table and sat down next to Millie. "We do have a double murder on our hands," she spoke in a solemn voice. "Millie is right: Young Greenson didn't kill himself." Michelle sipped on her coffee. "We found a whiskey bottle in Mr. Potter's trailer with Mr. Greenson's fingerprints on it. The whiskey bottle was not present during my initial examination of the trailer."

"Someone planted the whiskey bottle, then," Sam said and grabbed the last mug of coffee and took a sip.

"That's right," Momma Peach told Sam. "We also found cane marks on the ground in front of poor Mr. Potter's trailer. The cane marks were fresh."

"And," Michelle added, "the officer in charge of guarding the trailer was lured away by Lindsey Sung, giving Mr. Hayman time to enter the trailer, plant the whiskey bottle, and get out without being seen."

Momma Peach took a sip of her fresh coffee. "The suicide note found on poor Mr. Greenson was nothing more than a fake note of confession claiming he killed Mr. Potter in a fit of jealous rage. Of course, that's horseradish, and we all know it."

Millie soaked in the new information, shocked that such confidential information was being made public in her presence. Then her mind understood why. "You two are wondering if I know more than I'm letting on, right?" she asked.

"Do you, honey?" Momma Peach asked.

"You mean do I know more about Mr. Hayman and his black cat?" Millie asked.

"Yes," Michelle answered in a calm voice. "Millie, any information you have about Mr. Hayman and Miss Sung would be valuable at this point. Mr. Hayman's attorney is arriving tomorrow and as of right now, I have no ammunition to fight with. My back is in a corner and I have no choice but to let the circus leave town. If the circus leaves town...the killer will get away clean and free."

Millie sipped her coffee. The coffee was the best she had ever tasted, but it couldn't distract her from the sick feeling in her stomach at the thought of Lionel Hayman. "All I know about Mr. Hayman is that he's a snob of a man with ice in his veins."

"Back at the circus, you said Mr. Potter thought there was some good in Mr. Hayman. Why?" Momma Peach asked.

"Oh, Lance tried to find good in a rattlesnake," Millie said in a frustrated tone. "He was always trying to buddy up to Mr. Hayman and make that miserable man smile.

Whenever he could, Lance would always sneak over to the snake den and try to talk with the head cobra himself. I always warned Lance that he was fighting a losing battle, but he never listened to me. For some reason, Lance was determined to make friends with Mr. Hayman. It was like..." Millie pondered her thoughts. "It was like Lance was trying to rescue a lost child locked in a man's body. Only the lost child was a snake, but Lance could never see that. He always sought the good in people."

Momma Peach took a sip of coffee, closed her eyes, and saw a kind man who desired peace and love over hate and violence. "Not many men like Lance Potter left in the world," she sighed. "I think your Mr. Potter would have gotten along with our Mr. Sam—he's like that, too. A rare breed."

Millie looked at Sam. She could plainly see goodness in the man. "Sam, can I ask you a favor?"

"Sure."

"Well, I don't like being parked on the street, as nice as it is. I need a temporary campground," Millie explained. "Momma Peach wants me to stay with her but, well...my RV is my home."

"And you want to know if you can park your RV here at the farm?" Sam asked. Millie nodded. "Sure, there's plenty of space to park an RV. As a matter of fact, you can back your RV into the barn and I can run an electrical cord out to you."

Millie smiled in relief. "Thank you, Sam. That would be very nice."

Momma Peach smiled at Michelle. Michelle nodded. "Well," Momma Peach said, "for now, let's focus on supper and let the shadows sleep. There will be plenty of time to fuss with shadows tomorrow."

As they turned to easier talk of supper, Millie felt grateful that Momma Peach let the subject of the murders drop. Even though she felt very sad inside—she also felt very afraid. Whoever killed Young Greenson might come after her simply because she knew him. His killer might believe she had some type of secret information that might be dangerous. "Dinner sounds good to me," Millie said and looked back at Sam. "I drove my RV over, Sam. Maybe after dinner, you can help me back my RV into your barn?"

"Sure thing," Sam promised. "The barn is a bit dusty, but tomorrow I'll get out there and clean up."

"I'll help," Millie promised. "You know, the thought of cleaning up an old barn makes me feel right at home. I grew up on a ranch outside of Dallas, and cleaning barns is as natural as breathing air to me," she told Sam.

"I figured as much," Sam replied. "You have that look."

"You sure do," Momma Peach agreed.

"Absolutely," Michelle added. "I bet you can ride a horse blindfolded, too."

"Well," Millie blushed, "I am an expert rider." Millie put down her coffee. "I still own the family ranch where I grew up back in Texas. Oh, the ranch isn't what it used to be. I kept up the old house, but I don't run cattle and sell horses anymore like I did in my younger days, so the barn is probably just as dusty as you can imagine."

Momma Peach took a sip of her coffee and began to ask Millie what type of horses she sold when an idea struck her mind. "Melanie," she exclaimed.

"The elephant?" Millie asked, confused.

"Yes," Momma Peach said in an excited voice. She turned to Sam. "Mr. Sam, you have lots of land."

"A few dozen acres, sure," Sam replied in a confused voice. Then his mind latched onto the light in Momma Peach's eyes. "Oh no, what are you up to, Momma Peach?"

Michelle knew. "Melanie needs a new home, Sam. And Lidia needs money to buy Melanie."

"Lidia was fired today," Momma Peach explained.

"An elephant...on my land?" Sam swallowed nervously.

"Hey now, I can take care of horses, but an elephant...I wouldn't even know what to feed an elephant."

Millie felt excitement course through her heart. "Hey, I can give Lidia the money she needs to buy Melanie, and Sam, if you're willing, Melanie could just stay on your land until we find her a permanent home. Oh, she's such a sweet baby. Harmless and gentle."

Sam looked into the faces of three desperately hopeful women. What could he say? "I guess I'm going to need lots of hay." He looked a little dazed at the thought.

"Oh, thank you, Mr. Sam." Momma Peach hurried over to Sam and wrapped her loving arms around him. "The thought of letting that old buzzard Lionel Hayman steal that elephant away from the woman who loves and cares for her was sure making me sick to my stomach."

"Lidia is a good woman, Sam. You'll like her. She's a Texan like me. As a matter of fact, most of the people working for Mr. Hayman are from the Dallas area."

"Really?" Michelle asked.

Millie nodded. "Dallas is the headquarters for Mr. Hayman and his black cat," Millie said and sighed. "At least now, Lidia and Melanie will be able to be free of them. Assuming Mr. Hayman sells Melanie, which I think he will. That man hates elephants. As you saw, Melanie is the only elephant that belongs to the circus. The poor dear deserves to be free."

Michelle took a sip of her coffee and began thinking. Momma Peach joined her. But instead of asking questions, both women filed their questions away in silence and focused on supper. "Sam," Momma Peach said, "as much as I hate to say this...let's eat."

Sam nodded. "I'm starved," he admitted and then caught his words. "I mean, I may be hungry...and maybe this food might be suitable for supper..." Sam cast his eyes down at the floor and hurried over to the table.

Momma Peach shook her head. "Uh huh," she said and nodded, "I have a ship full of traitors in this here kitchen."

Michelle couldn't help but grin at Momma Peach. "Well, Momma Peach," she said, "we survived lunch. Maybe we'll survive dinner?"

Momma Peach walked over the stove and peeked into the oven. She had to admit that the pumpkin pie sure smelled good. "Maybe we won't end up in the emergency room," she fussed and closed the oven. She turned and pointed a finger at Sam. "Next time I'm going to set an alarm clock right beside your head, Mr. Sam."

Sam winked at Millie. Millie smiled. It felt nice to be in a room full of decent folk who meant well toward her. "Let's eat," she said and then added for Momma Peach's benefit: "If we can, that is. Such awful food might be hard to get down."

Momma Peach smiled. "That's my girl."

Far away in the darkness of the night, Lindsey Sung slunk across the fairgrounds, slipping into the shadows of a striped tent and disappearing as stealthily as a cat. Clouds dripped low above the peaked tents and the moon vanished behind the heavy cloud cover, plunging the circus into darkness.

*M*omma Peach watched Michelle meet Lionel at the front entrance to the main tent. Lindsey Sung stood beside him with an evil expression on her face. "That's Lindsey Sung," Momma Peach told Old Joe.

Old Joe leaned forward in the backseat of Michelle's car with a tasty cinnamon roll in one hand and a cup of coffee in the other. He looked at Lindsey and whistled. "What is it, you old fox?" Momma Peach scowled.

"That woman is mighty cute," Old Joe told Momma Peach and took a good bite of his cinnamon roll.

"And very deadly, you back-alley tomcat," Momma Peach said and slapped at Old Joe to make him lean back in his seat. "I ain't in no mood for you to have your head turned around by a pretty face. That's exactly what got the deputy in trouble. She knows she can turn heads. Don't be a dummy like the last man."

Old Joe rolled his eyes. "Sure, Momma Peach," he said and pointed at a thin East Asian man with straight black hair wearing a conservative black suit. "Who is that?"

Momma Peach studied Lionel Hayman's attorney with careful, patient eyes through a white morning mist that had settled in over the fairgrounds. "That man has to be Mr. Hayman's attorney. Seems like the man arrived sooner than expected." He looked to be of Chinese ancestry, like Lindsey.

"What do we do now?" Old Joe asked. He took a sip of his coffee and watched Michelle fold her arms. Michelle was obviously becoming impatient. She pointed into the tent. Lionel hesitated and then nodded. Although Lionel, his attorney, and Lindsey were clearly unhappy about it, they turned and led Michelle into the tent.

"Okay, she's lured the guilty out of sight. It's our turn now," Momma Peach told Old Joe. She turned around in the front passenger seat and looked Old Joe in the face. Old Joe appeared sleepy and tired in his brown rain jacket, but Momma Peach still saw a hint of clear brilliance in the man's eyes. "I need you at your best, you old fox. Can I count on you?"

"I'm here, ain't I?" Old Joe asked and quickly polished off his cinnamon roll and drained the remainder of his coffee. "I ain't gonna betray you no more, Momma Peach. You can count on me, yes sir and yes ma'am."

Momma Peach felt a smile touch her lips. "I reckon I can," she said and quickly eased out of the front seat and stepped into the heavy mist. Old Joe followed. "Follow me," Momma Peach whispered and on her short but stealthy legs, she eased around the main tent and aimed her body toward Lionel Hayman's trailer. Old Joe followed, casting his hawk eyes around, absorbing every little detail of the circus grounds, every tent, trailer, cage, bale of hay, sound, and smell. The circus was silent, sleepy and still, but Old Joe was pretty certain that all the circus folk wasn't snoring away in their lumpy beds; no sir. He was grateful for the white mist, which allowed some cover. But Old Joe also knew that as soon as the sun warmed up, the mist would be burned away. "Momma Peach, we have no more than thirty minutes," he whispered.

Momma Peach passed Melanie's cage. Melanie was lying down with her eyes closed. Momma Peach paused, stared at the beautiful elephant, sighed, and then moved on. "I will be back for you."

"Where are the cops?" Old Joe asked.

"Michelle pulled our folks back early this morning. She

77

wants to give our snakes a false sense of victory," Momma Peach explained. She pointed to Lionel's trailer. "There it is. Let's get our old legs moving."

"I am moving," Old Joe promised. He felt a surge of excitement jolt through his body. Suddenly he felt young, alive and full of energy—he felt like his old self, preparing to pull off the biggest scam in the history of the State of Georgia. Of course, he knew he was nothing more than an old, washed-up conman breaking into a circus trailer, but so what? Adrenaline kicked in no matter how silly the job.

Momma Peach eased up to Lionel's trailer and stopped. Water was dripping off her gray rain jacket. Momma Peach had chosen the color gray in order to appear less conspicuous against the tents and the muddy, misty field. She felt like a brave spy engaged in a dangerous mission behind enemy lines. "Wait," she whispered and pulled out two pairs of garden gloves from the right pocket of her rain jacket. "I don't want to be leaving fingerprints."

Old Joe looked at the garden gloves, rolled his eyes, and pulled out a pair of stealthier looking black gloves from the front pocket of his gray trousers. "I work in style."

"You better get this door unlocked before I beat that style out of your head to make room for some sense," Momma Peach warned old Joe and slapped on a pair of garden gloves and shoved the extra pair back into the pocket of her rain jacket. Old Joe flinched, threw on his gloves, and went to work.

The door to Lionel's trailer was obviously locked, but the lock was mere candy to Old Joe. The aged conman pulled a thief's lockpick tool from his front pocket and went to work. Less than sixty seconds later he replaced the tool in his pocket and eased open the front door. "Ladies first," he smiled.

"You're gonna tell me where you got that little doodad of a gadget later," Momma Peach warned Old Joe and hurried into the trailer. She stepped into an extremely neat trailer decorated as fancy as a business office. A glossy wooden desk was shoved up against the far corner. Two wooden filing cabinets sat on the right side of the desk, resting on a lush Persian carpet. A fax machine and a copy machine stood a few feet away from the desk, ready for use. A simple kitchen and sleeping area stared at the desk from the opposite side of the trailer, neat and tidy. Momma Peach would have been impressed at the sight of such neatness, but she knew the man occupying the trailer was either a killer or harboring a killer, and not a man to be applauded for keeping a nice home.

Old Joe stepped into the trailer and closed the front door. "Hey, classy," he said and whistled.

"Classy my foot," Momma Peach fussed. She pointed at the two filing cabinets. "There has to be a safe in here somewhere. Go find it."

Old Joe nodded and began walking toward the bed. Momma Peach watched with urgent eyes. "Ain't no man gonna keep a safe in his business area...at least not in a set-up like this," Old Joe told Momma Peach and rubbed his chin. He slowly began tapping the carpet with his right foot. "Let's see here...this trailer is modern...well-built...can hold a good amount of floor weight..." Old Joe kept tapping the floor with his foot. "We walked up four steps to get inside this here trailer, which means there's space underneath our feet and—" Old Joe felt his right foot strike an odd piece of flooring under the carpet, very close to the bed. "Ah," he said and eased down on his knees and began feeling the carpet with his hands. A minute later he pulled back a flap of carpet and pointed to the door of a small, gray metal safe that had been embedded into the floor.

Momma Peach hurried over to the safe and looked down. "I will cook you one of my famous peach pies," she said in a pleased voice.

"Letting me stay in your home is reward enough," Old Joe promised Momma Peach. "Now give me some air, Momma Peach. I have a safe to crack."

Momma Peach stepped back and watched Old Joe lower his ear to the safe and begin turning the safe dial. She expected the task of cracking the safe to take some time, but no more than five minutes passed before she heard a slight metallic *click* and she watched Old Joe pull the safe door open. "Well, I'll be," Momma Peach said in an amazed voice. "Why, you old fox."

Old Joe began to grin and then stopped. He grimaced in pain as he got to his knees and tried to get up. "Yeah, old fox is right," he sighed. Momma Peach offered him a hand to help him to a standing position. "I sure didn't put my talents to good use, I know that. I lost my best years chasing the worst the world had to offer, and my body tells me about it every day now."

Momma Peach patted Old Joe on his shoulder. "You're learning," she said and eased down onto her knees. "What's in the safe?"

"We don't have time to find out right now," Old Joe said, glancing out the window. "That mist will disappear any moment now and we'll lose our cover." She reached into the safe, yanked out a stack of brown folders and handed them to Old Joe, who shoved them into his jacket. He glanced down at a stack of money in the bottom of the safe, shook his head, and turned away, slamming the safe door shut with the toe of his shoe. "Let's go, Momma Peach."

Momma Peach nodded and stood back up. She watched Old Joe roll the carpet back down over the safe and then hurried outside. Old Joe followed on quick legs, but before exiting the trailer, he told her to go on ahead while he checked the desk drawers. He fiddled with the machines by the desk too while Momma Peach scanned around to make sure no one was approaching the trailer. Once outside, Old Joe followed Momma Peach through the mist, past Melanie's cage, and back to Michelle's car without being seen.

Old Joe crawled into the back seat and laughed to himself. "Job accomplished, Momma Peach."

Momma Peach closed the front passenger door and wiped sweat from her brow. "I thought for sure that Lindsey Sung was gonna pop up at any minute," she admitted. She turned and looked at Old Joe. "Baby, I sure am grateful you helped me."

"Ah, it was nothing. Piece of cake," Old Joe promised Momma Peach. He reached into his jacket, removed the files, and handed them to Momma Peach. "Still want to know where I got my little doodad gadget?" he grinned.

Momma Peach rolled her eyes. "Just as long as you only use that gadget as a toothpick, I guess it ain't none of my business anymore," Momma Peach said, taking the files from Old Joe. She began examining the contents. "These ain't circus papers," she grinned to herself. "No sir and no ma'am, these here papers are not circus papers at all."

Old Joe spotted Michelle walking out of the main tent. She jogged over to her car and jumped into the driver's seat. "Well?" she asked, wiping rainwater from her hair.

Momma Peach patted the folders in her lap. "Let's go back to your office."

Michelle looked down at the folders on Momma Peach's lap. "Hayman's attorney really tore into me. Vicious teeth on that one. I couldn't find any room to fight with him. As of now, I have no legal grounds to hold Hayman or his circus in town. Hayman has made it clear that he will be leaving the fairgrounds within the next eight hours."

"That should be plenty of time," Momma Peach told Michelle. "These here papers aren't circus papers." Momma Peach tossed a thumb at Old Joe. "That old fox did real good. He cracked open a hidden floor safe like nothing I have ever seen before."

"Wasn't nothing," Old Joe assured Michelle. "A man can train his ear to hear how a safe thinks, that's all."

Michelle looked at Old Joe through the rearview mirror. "Old Joe, if there's anything in those files that will help me hold Hayman in town I'm gonna buy you the biggest steak in...well, in Georgia." Michelle drew in a deep breath and got her car moving through the mist, pulling away from the deadly circus. "Of course, officially, I haven't the faintest idea where you picked up those files," she said with a wink at Momma Peach.

As she pulled away, Lionel walked Lindsey and his attorney back to his trailer. As soon as he unlocked the trailer door and stepped inside, he knew something was wrong. He ran over to the fax machine in a panic. "The fax, where is it?" he shouted.

Lindsey walked over to the fax machine and began checking the area. The fax was nowhere to be found. "The carpet is damp," she said running her hands over the carpet. "Someone has been in here."

Lionel brushed past Lindsey and made his way over to the floor safe. He dropped down onto his knees, yanked back the carpet and frantically opened the safe. "The files are gone!" he hollered and hit the floor with his fist. Lindsey stood very still. Lionel's attorney's face went pale. "The files are gone!"

"I'll go outside and begin questioning the employees. Perhaps someone witnessed the thieves?" Lindsey told Lionel.

Lionel raised his right hand at Lindsey. "If we don't find that fax and the files you might as well start running, Ms. Sung. You know as well as I do that if the fax and files are not located, everyone standing in this room will be killed." Lionel closed his eyes and drew in a deep breath, calming his panicked mind before he stood up. "Ms. Sung, go to the police station."

"Why?" Lindsey sputtered. "That cop couldn't be the thief."

"Detective Chan arrived with two people sitting in her car," Lionel hissed through gritted teeth.

"The fat old lady and that old man?" Lindsey asked. "Mr. Hayman, your panic is outweighing your common sense. This was clearly an inside job. One of the employees—"

"Those worthless idiots would not dare stand against me," Lionel spat out.

Lionel's attorney looked down at his shiny black shoes. Lionel was in serious trouble, which meant he was in serious trouble, too. But what could he do except run? So that's exactly what he did. He tore out of Lionel's trailer on shaky legs and didn't look back. Sure, he was dangerous in the courtroom, but there wasn't a courtroom in the world that could protect him from the organization that hired him to defend Lionel Hayman.

"Look at that coward run," Lionel said in a disgusted tone.

Lindsey stared at the fleeing man and watched him vanish into the mist. "He won't get far," she promised and focused her attention back on Lionel. "Mr. Hayman, surely this was an inside job. I'll go question our employees...with certain force...and extract the truth."

Lionel stared at Lindsey. The woman seemed calm in the face of certain annihilation. Why? "Are you disobeying a direct order, Ms. Sung?"

"No, Mr. Hayman," Lindsey said. "I'm simply stating that I do not believe two senile retirees could have broken into this trailer and removed files from a safe that is strong enough to withstand a nuclear war. It's impossible, Mr.

Hayman, unless the thief has the combination to the safe," Lindsey shook her head. "Don't you get it? It's someone who knows the combination."

Lionel considered Lindsey's statement. "I suppose you're right," he caved and slowly walked back to the fax machine, retrieved his cane, and turned to face Lindsey. "Yes, of course," he finally said, "the thief must be one of our employees. Please, go conduct your questioning."

Lindsey nodded and walked outside into the mist. Surely, she thought, the thief had to be working for her. Surely Momma Peach and Old Joe couldn't have broken into the trailer and cracked a sophisticated safe, right? "We'll soon find out," Lindsey growled and made her way toward Lidia's trailer.

Momma Peach slapped Old Joe in the back of the head with her pocketbook. Poor Old Joe went flying out of Michelle's office and crashed into the hallway wall. "What did I say?" he asked and began rubbing the back of his head. "What did I do to deserve that, Momma Peach?"

"What did you do?" Momma Peach asked with anger flaming as hot as lava in her eyes. She eased out into the hallway. Old Joe swallowed and began backing away. "What did you do, you old skunk?"

Old Joe knew he was in trouble. "All I did was ask this here police department to show me some gratitude by greasing my palms with some dough."

Michelle sighed, shook her head, and watched Momma Peach take a swing at Old Joe with her pocketbook. Old Joe ducked just in the nick of time. "You didn't ask nothing, you smelly alley cat! You demanded money!"

"Well...money is kinda tight, Momma Peach," Old Joe replied in a nervous voice. "I did them a favor and I just figured this here police department could spare a few bucks, is all."

"Michelle already offered to buy you a nice steak dinner, but was that enough? Noooo," Momma Peach said and took a third swing at Old Joe. Old Joe ducked and ran. "I'll deal with you at home!" Momma Peach yelled.

Old Joe scooted away, forgetting all about the fax in his pocket. When he managed to reach fresh air, he glanced over his shoulder from the wet parking lot, searching for Momma Peach, and then sighed. "That woman's temper will be the death of me for sure," he said. "But why should I be surprised? I ain't no saint." Old Joe let his shoulders sag and walked away.

Back in Michelle's office, Momma Peach tossed her pocketbook down onto the desk and plopped down in a chair. "Just when I think Old Joe is learning to be decent," she huffed, her heart heavy.

Michelle sat down behind her desk and picked up one of the folders Old Joe had managed to take from Lionel's floor safe. "Give him more time, Momma Peach. Old dogs can't learn new tricks overnight. Besides, Old Joe did save the day," she pointed out and nodded at the folder in her hand.

"I just wish that old skunk would learn that a decent, honest living is worth a shot," Momma Peach sighed. "Old Joe needs family love. But he ain't willing to let folk in enough to trust them. It's a shame, too, because I know that Old Joe has goodness in him. That man isn't getting a day younger and unless he settles his mind and heart he's just gonna fall into a deeper pit."

Michelle saw a strained worry in Momma Peach's eyes. Momma Peach was sincerely worried about the old conman. Not romantically, of course—but the way a sister worries about her lost brother. Old Joe wasn't the type of man anyone else would concern themselves with, Michelle knew, and maybe that's why Momma Peach was stepping into the ring. "Give him time, Momma Peach."

Momma Peach looked at Michelle. She saw care and warmth on Michelle's face, which comforted her tired heart. "Mandy and Rosa might lock him in the cellar again if I give that old skunk too much time."

Michelle smiled. "Speaking of Mandy and Rosa, those

two girls are really doing a wonderful job managing your bakery."

"My sweet babies sure are pulling long hours for my sake," Momma Peach beamed. "I slipped them both a very nice bonus in their recent paychecks, too. And of course," Momma Peach sighed, "they both tried to give back their bonuses, but I wouldn't let them. Mandy is dating that college fella now and Rosa is dating her childhood friend. My girls need money for nice clothes for dates and perfume...girly stuff."

"Mandy and Rosa are going out on a double date tomorrow night, if I remember correctly," Michelle told Momma Peach. "They're dating two nice enough guys."

"Oh, sure they are," Momma Peach agreed. "But the boys are not the fellas they're going to marry. I can tell. I see the look in the girls' eyes when they're around their little boyfriends. Not true, deep love. Just puppy love."

"Yeah, I caught that, too," Michelle nodded. "But Mandy and Rosa are still young. They both have time. Look how long it took for me to find love!" Michelle thought about Able, wondering if her boyfriend was thinking about her at the same exact moment. "Well, we better focus on the case, huh?"

Momma Peach reached across the desk and picked up a second folder. "Baby, Able will be home soon enough," she promised and opened the folder. "What we have here in these folders are evidence about illegal prescription drugs being smuggled through the circus."

"A regular black market," Michelle agreed. "The medicine being smuggled through the circus appears to be cancer medicines." Michelle studied the papers in the folder and a list on a notepad she had made, jotting down the usage of each unfamiliar drug. "The cancer drugs are smuggled into every major city in the United States and sold to the highest bidder."

Momma Peach raised a piece of brown paper in the air and pointed at it. "One million dollars for a single delivery of this medicine, maybe that's a couple dozen doses at most...and that's the lowest cost Momma Peach's eyes have seen so far."

Michelle studied the complex web of bank transfers outlined in the paperwork before them. "The proceeds are clearly going to shell companies that funnel the profits into campaign contributions...this one was sent to the America Forever PAC, that's a political action committee. But if you look closely, there's just hundreds of these PACs listed here. They're moving millions and millions and concealing the source and the amounts. These people are buying Washington, Momma Peach, plain and simple."

"Yep," Momma Peach said and continued to study the papers. "What we don't have here, are names. We have locations, dates, amounts, shell company lists, but no names."

"Names would have been helpful," Michelle agreed. "However, I have enough evidence here to keep the circus in town and Lionel Hayman and Lindsey Sung behind bars for a while. At least long enough to start questioning the people working at the circus. I'm sure some of them might talk once they see Lionel Hayman and Lindsey Sung are behind bars."

Momma Peach fished out a peppermint from her pocketbook and tossed it into her mouth. "I'm not happy. This political nonsense is one thing, but most of all, I don't like evil snakes hoarding good medicine that innocent folk need."

Michelle closed the folder in her hand and set it down on her desk. "Momma Peach, Lionel Hayman and Lindsey Sung are just the low-lifes at the bottom of the ladder. It's the bosses perched at the top that we have to worry about. We're dealing with power and money, Momma Peach." Michelle rubbed her cheek. "The people we're fighting against aren't worried about a small-town cop on their tail. They could easily erase me and you without blinking an eye."

"What are you trying to say?" Momma Peach asked Michelle in a worried voice. "Are you saying you want to back down from a fight?"

"Momma Peach, I have you to worry about, more than anyone. But I also have Able in my life now...and Sam, dear sweet Sam who is becoming like a daddy to me. And then there's Mandy and Rosa, too. Momma Peach, I love those girls," Michelle explained. "I could never forgive myself if anything ever happened to any one of you. I know the information we have sitting before us gives me enough legal power to arrest Lionel Hayman and Lindsey Sung and keep the circus in town...but if I do...who knows what might follow?"

Momma Peach understood Michelle's worry. "Baby, if we back off and let evil people sell healing medicine to other evil people while innocent babies suffer, why, I'd never be able to forgive myself."

"Momma Peach, the people we're up against will just find another channel to smuggle their medicine through," Michelle said in a fearful voice. She looked up at her friend and was stricken to see the look of surprise on Momma Peach's face. "Oh, Momma Peach, I'm sorry...I didn't mean to..." Michelle lowered her eyes in shame. "What am I saying? I'm putting my own personal fears and feelings before my job. I have a duty to perform, regardless of the dangers."

"That's right. Now you raise those pretty eyes and look up at me." Michelle raised her eyes and looked at Momma Peach. "You're a fighter. Never forget that. And never forget that I am proud of you, no matter what. You could throw your towel into the ring right now and I would dance praises around you. So don't you ever—and I mean ever—think bad of your precious self, because I know the truth."

Michelle felt honor wash through her heart. "Thank you, Momma Peach." Michelle drew in a deep breath and then grabbed her phone and picked it up to dial. "Yes, this is Detective Chan, get me Judge Morris."

Momma Peach beamed. "That's my girl."

Three hours later, Michelle arrived at the circus with a squad of police officers and all the warrants she needed to take care of business. She walked toward Lionel Hayman's trailer under a clear blue sky blowing with autumn's wind.

Lionel was standing near his trailer with Lindsey Sung at his side. Lindsey had been unsuccessful in pealing any useful information from the employees, which left his hands tied. He certainly couldn't pull the circus down and run before locating and retrieving his stolen papers. Then he saw Michelle walking toward him with a squad of police officers, and he knew the tent was about to fall for good.

"Lionel Hayman and Lindsey Sung," Michelle said in a tough cop tone, "I am placing you both under arrest." Michelle presented a copy of the arrest warrants and handed them to Lionel and Lindsey. "Officer Barnett, read them their Miranda Rights and haul them out of here."

Lindsey narrowed her eyes and stared at Michelle. "We'll continue our fight," she promised.

"Anytime," Michelle whispered. "But first I'm going to get justice for two dead men who didn't deserve to die."

Lionel felt his stomach turn weak. "There has been a misunderstanding," he said, attempting to keep his voice calm and cool. "My attorney will not be pleased."

"Where is your attorney, Mr. Hayman?" Michelle asked and glanced around. But the man only sputtered and had no reply.

As Michelle looked around just then, she spotted Lidia standing near the elephant, Melanie. From what she could see, it appeared that Lidia was holding a shaky hand over her right eye. She quickly jogged over to Lidia and gently pulled the woman's hand away from her eye. An ugly, dark bruise appeared. "Who struck you?"

Lidia fought back tears. "I can't say," she answered in a trembling voice. "Please, my life is in danger." Lidia turned away from Michelle and focused on the elephant lying on the straw next to her. "Melanie's life has been threatened, too. If I talk, Melanie will be killed."

Michelle gazed at the reclining elephant, whose large eyes were sad and depressed. The sweet elephant obviously knew her trainer's life was in danger. "Lindsey Sung struck you, didn't she?"

Lidia didn't answer. Michelle gently touched the scared woman's shoulder. "Please," Lidia begged, "I have to think about Melanie."

"I'm shutting this circus down, you're safe now," Michelle told Lidia and pointed at Momma Peach, who was standing in the distance near the main tent. "Melanie is going to be fine. We even found her a home and Millie Frost is going to give you the money to buy Melanie," Michelle explained. "But I have a feeling you won't need to buy Melanie now."

Lidia slowly turned and faced Michelle. "What are you talking about, Detective Chan?"

"I'll explain—"

"Hey!" A police officer yelled in a loud voice.

Michelle spun around and saw Lindsey Sung kick Officer Barnett in the chest and then sidekick a second police officer in the face; both police officers went crashing down to the ground like bags of wet sand. Before anyone else could react, Lindsey grabbed Lionel and stood him between herself and the remaining officers. She then kicked his chest so that he was shoved into the officers, knocking them all over, and used the momentum from the kick to flip backward and twist nimbly in the air. She landed, took off at a sprint and vanished around the side of Lionel's trailer.

Michelle didn't waste a second. She dashed forward on legs like lightning and chased after Lindsey. When she ran around Lionel's trailer, she saw Lindsey jumping a fence located in the far rear of the fairgrounds. Thick woods lay beyond the fence. "We'll continue our battle, cop!" Lindsey yelled at Michelle and ran off into the woods.

"Maybe sooner than you think," Michelle said, running to the fence and preparing to jump over it. But then she paused. Something in her gut warned her to stay out of the woods. Michelle clutched the fence and stared into the unknown with adrenaline and anger pumping in her veins. The woods suddenly changed from innocent, South Georgia woods into a dark, untamed forest filled with silent enemies. "Run, girl," Michelle whispered and walked away.

She found Momma Peach standing beside Melanie. "Lindsey Sung has escaped," she said in a worried voice and threw a glance at Officer Barnett. She wanted to scold the man but knew better. Lindsey Sung was a trained, skilled assassin and he was a simple cop with a few extra pounds sagging over his belt. Officer Barnett slapped a pair of handcuffs on Lionel and looked down at the ground in shame. The other officers were wiping grass and mud off their uniforms from when Lindsey Sung had knocked them over in the fight.

"Baby," Momma Peach told Melanie, "you're going to stay with me. Later, when Detective Chan gives the green light, I will have Mr. Sam come and fetch our sweet Melanie in a trailer, okay?"

Lidia was too tired to argue. Her mind was focused on Melanie's wellbeing. "Okay," she said. "I don't really have much money right now. A kind favor like that would be nice."

Momma Peach looked at Michelle. Michelle was staring at Officer Barnett as he walked Lionel Hayman over to the patrol car. "How bad is it?" she asked.

"Lindsey Sung isn't leaving town anytime soon," Michelle warned Momma Peach. "That woman is a hired killer. She'll die before she abandons a mission." Michelle slowly drifted her eyes over to Momma Peach. "Lindsey Sung isn't going to leave until we're all dead," she promised.

Momma Peach felt a cold chill walk down her spine. "Baby, surely not—"

"Momma Peach," Michelle interrupted, "we're all sitting targets now," she said and walked over to talk to Lionel Hayman through the open door of the squad car where he sat, handcuffed. "If you want to live, you better start talking, pal."

"If I talk, I'm dead," Lionel spat in contempt. "Please do tell your goons not to forget my cane, will you?"

"Get him downtown," Michelle told Officer Barnett and walked into Lionel's trailer. A few moments later, Momma Peach joined her. "Momma Peach, we're in some very serious trouble. I wasn't counting on Lindsey Sung escaping."

Momma Peach stood very still and looked around the trailer. The circus was in town, but the main event wasn't very funny. No sir and no ma'am, the main event wasn't funny at all.

CHAPTER FIVE

*M*omma Peach examined a pink and white clown costume. The clown costume was vintage silk and very valuable. "That was my very first costume," an old man's voice spoke up in a thick Russian accent. Momma Peach lifted her right finger and ran it down the sleeve of the costume. Images of black and white circus days whispered through her mind as wonderful circus music played, filled with the smell of popcorn and the sounds of laughing children. "The old days are gone."

"Yes, they are," Momma Peach agreed. She turned away from the costume and focused her eyes on Max Moroz. Max Moroz gazed back at Momma Peach with a large cigar in his mouth and a head full of thin gray hair. The old man was small, thin and appeared very sickly. His wrinkled face was very pale and his eyes bloodshot. Yet he somehow managed to appear very intelligent in the simple blue silk shirt he wore over a pair of tailored brown trousers. "Did Mr. Hayman or Lindsey Sung kill Mr. Potter and Mr. Greenson?" she asked in a respectful voice.

Max remained sitting on the brown sofa in his small trailer. His trailer was filled with old world circus antiques from the old days—each relic preserved with loving hands; hands that were old and wrinkled now, but still moved with the same love. "Yes and no," he told Momma Peach. "One man was killed for a reason you do not expect, and the other man was killed for a reason you do expect."

Momma Peach nodded. She pointed to a wooden chair stationed close to the couch. "May I sit down?"

"Please."

Momma Peach settled herself in the chair. "Mr. Moroz—"

"Call me Max," Max told Momma Peach and puffed on his cigar. "My mother was a performer perhaps, the same as me. She presented me with a very interesting stage name, no? Mister Max Moroz?"

Momma Peach watched cigar smoke float in the air. The smoke smelled expensive and cozy. "Yes," Momma Peach smiled, realizing that a Mr. Max Moroz without a cigar would seem very strange. "Max, talk to me. By now you know Lindsey Sung—"

"Awful creature," Max stated.

"Yes, she is," Momma Peach agreed. "That awful creature has escaped."

Max worked on his cigar. "Lindsey Sung," he said in a calm voice, "is a killer. Yes."

"Did she kill Mr. Potter?"

"No," Max answered.

"Did she kill Mr. Greenson?"

"Yes," Max answered. "During the night, I saw her enter his trailer. I have very clear eyes. Good eyesight, all my life."

Momma Peach steadied herself. "You didn't actually see Lindsey Sung kill Mr. Greenson, though, right?"

"My soul felt her kill that man," Max explained and tapped his heart.

Momma Peach nodded. She had no doubt that Lindsey Sung was the person who killed poor Mr. Greenson, rest his soul. She wasn't sure how Michelle would present Mr. Max's soul as evidence to a judge, however. "Do you know who killed Mr. Potter?"

"Yes."

"Talk to me," Momma Peach told Max in a caring voice. "I am searching for answers."

Max Moroz stared at Momma Peach through heavy cigar smoke. "Mr. Potter was a very fine, skilled performer."

"I'm sure the poor man was."

"The person who killed Mr. Potter is very clever, yes?"

Momma Peach shrugged her shoulders. "I don't think no killer is above the law."

"Ah, the law," Max said and grinned. "The laws men chain themselves to."

Momma Peach made a funny face. For a mere second, Max almost sounded like Lindsey Sung. "You are a clown. You worked with Mr. Potter and—"

"I supervised," Max corrected Momma Peach. "My days of performing are over, yes?"

"I'm very sorry to hear that."

Max nodded and puffed on his cigar. "Age is not an enemy that we can escape from," he explained. "I am seventy-five years old and have over fifty years of my life performing for others as a simple clown. Two years ago, my body forced me to quit."

Momma Peach heard bitterness in Max's voice. "Retiring can be very difficult."

"Yes, it can," Max agreed and then grew very silent and puffed on his cigar. The cigar smoke drifted around clown costumes, a vintage makeup table that he told her had been hand-carved in Ukraine, plastic tubes of face paint, red rubber noses, colorful scarves, worn-out clown shoes, silly masks, and other items that mingled with the life of a clown like old friends. "I was one of the greats in Russia," Max finally spoke.

"Oh?" Momma Peach asked.

"Yes," Max stated in a very serious, proud voice. "The name of Max Moroz was respected among every performer. When I entered the ring to perform, every eye turned, envious of my skills." Max closed his eyes. "I was Max Moroz, the Great Clown of Comedy. The Greatest Performer, they called me. No other man could match my skill."

"If you were successful in Russia, what brought you to America?" Momma Peach asked.

Max opened his eyes with anger and sadness. "I was shamed," he whispered. "Many years ago, I was brought to disgrace by a group of men who were jealous of me. These men conspired to ruin me...and succeeded. I was forced to flee in...disgrace."

"What happened?" Momma Peach asked Max.

Max closed his eyes again. "I am a man who drinks only water," he explained. "I drank a gallon of water each day.

But I have never allowed liquor to touch my lips." Max shook his head with pain. "I prided myself on my strength, but I admit at times I became...a little fatigued. So before some performances, I would self-administer a vitamin shot. Just Vitamin B, you understand. Nothing illegal," he hastened to add. "It was all prescribed by my doctor, in fact."

"Keep going," Momma Peach told Max.

"The men who conspired to destroy me replaced my vitamin shot that night with alcohol. I became very intoxicated and shamed myself," Max confessed in a sad voice. "I have very little memory of that awful night, yet, I was told I even...insulted innocent children."

Momma Peach nodded. "Mr. Greenson concealed liquor in Mr. Potter's drink before a performance."

"Yes, I know," Max told Momma Peach. "I saw Mr. Greenson do so."

"Oh?"

"Yes," Max said, "but I did nothing. Why? Because I was jealous of Lance Potter."

"Why?"

"Because Lance Potter was the only man who matched my skill...not only matched...but defeated. When I saw Mr. Greenson place poison into his drink, I did nothing, simply because I wanted Lance Potter to face disgrace,"

Max explained. "Does that make me a cruel man? Perhaps it does. Jealousy is a very ugly cancer."

Momma Peach bit down on her lower lip. Max Moroz was becoming creepier in her mind. Her warm impression of a tired but genteel old man was quickly cooling with the smell of danger. "Why did you ask me to speak with you?" she asked Max.

"Mr. Max Moroz does not like cops," Max stated, smiling faintly. "I also have a conscience, even though I do not like the law." Max placed his cigar into a metal ashtray sitting beside him on the couch. Then he leaned forward and picked up a gallon jug full of water and took a drink. "It is good to drink water, yes?"

"Yes," Momma Peach said and waited.

Max took another drink of water and then put down the plastic jug. "I am a man of conscience," he repeated and looked into Momma Peach's eyes. "Do you understand these words?" he asked.

"I am beginning to think that I do," Momma Peach said and slowly wrapped her hand around the strap of her pocketbook. "You killed poor Mr. Potter."

Max locked his cold eyes on Momma Peach. "If that is so, then you must prove your accusation, yes? A man would be insane to confess guilt...yet he would be guilty if he did not have a conscience, yes?"

Momma Peach stood up. "Don't play games with me, you rotten old skunk!" she warned. "It's been over two weeks since I have had a rest from this bedeviled circus and I ain't in no mood to play games with the likes of you! Oh, give me strength, give me strength, the circus is in town and I am dealing with some peachy folks."

Max remained calm. He retrieved his cigar and took a puff. "You are an investigator, yes?"

"You bet your backside Momma Peach is an investigator," she retorted. "But more than anything, I am a human being with a heart for justice, you miserable old worm."

Max waved away Momma Peach's insult. "I come to you as a man with a conscience. If I am guilty of ending the life of an innocent man, then perhaps you will chain me to my guilt and soothe my conscience. If you fail, then perhaps my own conscience will be my eternal prison, yes?" Max puffed on his cigar, in a philosophical mood. "So I suppose you must begin your work."

"I'll clobber you, is what I'll do!" Momma Peach promised and nearly wound up her arm to smack Max around his trailer with her pocketbook. But instead, she remained in place and forced her brain to absorb the situation. Max Moroz killed Lance Potter, rest his poor soul, and not Lionel Hayman or Lindsey Sung. However, Lionel Hayman and Lindsey Sung saw a door of opportunity with Mr. Greenson and used the man's death to create a way out for the circus. And why not? Being trapped in a small Georgia town wasn't good for business, right? Not at all. Lionel Hayman and Lindsey Sung had a black market to run, so what was the death of one man if it meant clearing the circus for travel?

"Your assault on my body is nothing compared to the pain a man with a conscience is consumed with," Max told Momma Peach. "So please, get to work, and see what clues you might discover. I'll remain here at the circus."

Momma Peach stared at Max. What a world she was living in. A world where people were going more berserk by the second. "I am going to take you down, old man," she promised and walked outside into a cool evening. "Oh, give me strength, give me strength," she whispered.

Michelle spotted Momma Peach and hurried over to her with a cup of coffee in hand. "Well, what did Mr. Moroz have to say?" she asked.

"What did that old man have to say?" Momma Peach asked Michelle and then rolled her eyes. "Baby, that old man just about confessed to me that he killed poor Mr. Potter, rest his soul."

"What?" Michelle asked in a shocked voice.

Momma Peach nodded. "His wording was very clever, so I don't recommend arresting him. He said it without saying it. You wouldn't have any legal ground to hold him on." Momma Peach looked at Michelle. "Max Moroz has challenged me to a game. He wants me to capture him, which means..." Momma Peach rubbed her chin, "which means there must be a hidden clue somewhere in this circus."

Michelle looked around. The circus grounds were silent. No one dared to leave their trailers. No one dared to speak to the law, save Mr. Moroz. And no one dared to mention the name of Lionel Hayman or Lindsey Sung. "This place is really spooky, Momma Peach. These people...they're like...these strange twilight zone-type people, you know? You'd think that with Lionel Hayman in custody and Lindsey Sung on the run, one of them might open up and talk now."

Momma Peach felt the eerie mood slithering about in the air. "Baby, these people are scared, not strange. But there is a killer among them, and I have to catch that killer."

Michelle thought back to the dark, foggy night when Mr. Moroz committed the crime. In her imagination, the circus was quiet. The grounds were empty and still. Suddenly, Max Moroz slipped out of his trailer unseen, eased through the heavy fog like a dark shadow hunting for prey, knocked on the door of Lance Potter's trailer, entered, and then...struck. They had already searched all these areas, however, so where was this mysterious clue?

"Momma Peach, if you think Max Moroz confessed to you that he killed Lance Potter, then I'll arrest him and hold him. Who knows, maybe he'll break and make a confession."

"Max Moroz has issued a challenge. I know better than to think he'll break sitting in a run-down interrogation room, too. No, that man is brilliant and deadly. He wants me to capture him, but he sure ain't gonna roll out the red carpet, either."

"Momma Peach, we have Lindsey Sung to worry about. We don't have time to play games with a deranged old man."

"Baby, that man isn't deranged. He's just as deadly in his old age as he was in his young age," Momma Peach explained and took Michelle's coffee from her hand. "No sir and no ma'am," she said, taking a sip of coffee and nearly spit it out. "Oh, too much sugar."

Michelle took back her coffee. "I know," Michelle apologized. "Next time I'll make my own coffee instead of having one brought in to me." Michelle looked at Max Moroz's trailer. She saw the old man peer out at her from behind a curtain and then vanish again as the curtain fell back into place. "I'll run a check on him."

"I was hoping you would. In the meantime, I have to search these here grounds for whatever clue Max Moroz has hidden for me to find," Momma Peach explained. She looked toward Lance Potter's trailer. "I am going to have to go back into that poor man's trailer."

Before Michelle could answer, Millie came running up. "Okay, Sam is here with the trailer. We can take

Melanie now. He's also coming to grips with my canine friends. I guess I should have mentioned all of them at dinner last night." Millie looked at Michelle. "Are we clear?"

"You're clear, Millie," Michelle told Millie. "You're clear. I've called the mayor and informed him of the situation. He's ordering a special permit that you can pick up tomorrow morning down at the city hall. Tell Sam to be there bright and early, okay?"

"I will," Millie promised. She began to jog away but stopped. Something in Michelle's eyes worried her. "Do you really think Lindsey Sung will try something?" she asked. "That woman could be miles from here by now."

"Millie," Michelle said and pointed toward the woods behind the fairgrounds, "Lindsey Sung works for very powerful men. She is a woman determined to complete her mission regardless of the cost. She is also a woman who possesses great skill and resources. Lindsey Sung isn't worried about a small-town police department, and she's not worried about me. Her mission now is to kill anyone who may jeopardize the operation of her employers. Needless to say, I don't mean Mr. Lionel Hayman. I mean the men further up the chain."

Millie looked at Momma Peach. "That's right," Momma Peach told Millie. "Now you go help Lidia, bless her heart, get that sweet elephant out of here and tell Mr. Sam we'll be by later for supper." Momma Peach patted

Millie's hands. "And, don't let that man douse our supper with cayenne pepper."

"Sure," Millie forced a smile to her face and wandered away, leaving Momma Peach and Michelle trapped in a sticky web.

A heavy rain had settled in over the circus, causing the grounds to become saturated and muddy. Momma Peach sure wasn't interested in sneaking around a dark circus in a heavy rain, especially not with her belly full of one of Sam's full suppers that consisted of a very heavy chili dosed with enough cayenne pepper to scare off a coyote. "Oh, give me strength," Momma Peach moaned as she eased into the main tent wearing a black rain jacket, hoping the black jacket and hoodie would make her fade into the darkness without being seen by watchful eyes. Sure, there were a few cops roaming about in gray rain slickers, and sure, Momma Peach really didn't need to be sneaking around—however, being unseen was her mission. She didn't want even a tiny little field mouse knowing she was roaming about.

As Momma Peach eased through the darkness, a second figure appeared in the shadows and began walking toward Momma Peach with fierce power. Momma Peach didn't notice the figure. Instead, she hugged the right wall and began walking behind the bleachers, one slow step at a time. Surely, she thought, she would be able to find a secret position that would allow her to monitor Max Moroz. Surely, she would find a hiding spot, a safety net to think in. "Easy does it, girl," Momma Peach said, walking toward the far end of the main tent with her back pressed up against the canvas. "Mr. Sam's chili, cayenne pepper, and killers don't mix well together." Momma Peach paused, let out a painful burp, admonished Sam under her breath, and then continued on.

The dark figure watched Momma Peach and then dashed to the end of the main tent and waited. When Momma Peach reached the end of the tent, the figure slipped up behind Momma Peach and covered her mouth with a strong hand. "It's Michelle," Michelle whispered, "what in the world are you doing here, Momma Peach? I drove you home with Lidia."

Momma Peach nearly fainted. When Michelle let go of her mouth, she threw her hands over her chest. "Oh, I saw my life flash before my eyes," she whispered in a frantic voice. "Baby, you just scared me out of my wits."

"You told me you were going to wait until tomorrow to come back here because of the rain," Michelle insisted.

"I know," Momma Peach whispered, still breathing hard. And then, she farted. "Oh, give me strength. Mr. Sam's chili is going to cause the US Army to come running if I drop any more bombs."

Michelle waved her hands in front of her nose. "Oh, Momma Peach," she said.

"Blame Mr. Sam," Momma Peach complained and, against her will, let out a second fart. "Mercy, my stomach is really doing a number."

Michelle took a step back. "What are you doing here, Momma Peach?"

"Farting up a storm, it seems," Momma Peach whispered. "Shoo...give me strength, give me strength."

"I'm being serious," Michelle insisted. "You know Lindsey Sung is loose."

"I know," Momma Peach told Michelle and waited for her tummy to settle. "Hey, wait just a second. You told me you were spending the night in your office. What are you doing here, huh?" Michelle scuffed at the ground. "Oh, how the tables have turned."

"I came here hoping Lindsey Sung might show up," Michelle confessed.

"Well, I came back to this creepy place to watch Max Moroz's trailer," Momma Peach made her own confession. "There are four of your people prowling about. I didn't think I'd be in any danger."

"My men aren't a danger to Lindsey Sung," Michelle warned Momma Peach. "Lindsey Sung can kill my men within seconds if she chooses to."

"Don't I know it," Momma Peach said and stepped back and let out another fart. "Oh, Mr. Sam, what have you done to poor Momma Peach? Oh, give me strength, give me strength."

Michelle touched her own stomach. Sam's chili was a bit strong. "Well, since we're both here, we might as well work together, Momma Peach. We can watch Max Moroz's trailer from here and keep an eye out for Lindsey at the same time."

"Baby, do you think Lindsey Sung will show her face back here at this here circus?" Momma Peach asked as the damp night air bathed her face.

Michelle shrugged her shoulders. "She's somewhere, Momma Peach. My guess is she might be watching this circus as we speak."

Momma Peach bit down on her thumbnail. "Can you...what I mean is...can you—"

"Beat Lindsey Sung in a fight?" Michelle finished.

"Yes. Can...you?"

Michelle drew in a deep breath. "Momma Peach, I honestly don't know. Lindsey Sung is a skilled fighter and she doesn't look like she's lacking in discipline, either. That woman is, as you Southern people say, as fit as a fiddle. She sure isn't sitting around on her tush eating donuts like I've been doing."

Momma Peach made a pained face. Michelle was an agile fighter, but she did love her donuts. "What if Lindsey Sung wins the fight?" she dared to ask.

"Simple," Michelle stated, "she'll kill me, Momma Peach. Lindsey Sung isn't going to stop with only a few punches. Once she has me beaten down, she'll finish me off...lights out, so long, bye-bye, nice knowing you."

Momma Peach winced. "Oh, please tell me you have your gun on you," she begged.

"I do," Michelle promised, "but Momma Peach...I can't shoot Lindsey Sung. Lindsey and I will have to participate in hand-to-hand combat...she'll be expecting a gun, so she'll come at me so fast and so close the gun will be useless. When we fight...the last person standing...lives." Michelle reached out and touched Momma Peach's shoulder. "Don't feel bad for her, Momma Peach. If Lindsey Sung wins, she'll come after you next and then anyone else she might think is a danger to the men she is working for."

Momma Peach sighed and let her eyes soak in the vast space of the main tent. The tent was really dark. As far as she knew, Lindsey Sung could be crouched down and hiding in any shadow. "Okay, we'll take tonight one step at a time and see what happens," Momma Peach told Michelle and took her hand. "Let's find us a good hiding spot."

"Standing behind these bleachers is good," Michelle said. "The back flap is open, giving us a pretty good view of the tents and trailers."

Momma Peach looked out into the rain. She could see Max Moroz's trailer. "Okay, we'll stand here and wait. You didn't happen to bring any coffee with you, did you?"

"Coffee and Sam's chili don't mix well together, Momma Peach." Michelle rubbed her tummy again. She felt tired and worn-down. All she wanted to do was go home, cuddle up on the couch under a warm blanket with a bowl of hot, buttery popcorn, watch a movie, call Able, and then go to bed. Instead, she was standing in a dark, damp tent waiting for a deadly killer to appear and a sly old man to—maybe—slip out into the rain and make one false move. "Momma Peach, we need a vacation."

"Oh no," Momma Peach said and shook her head no. "Our last vacation we ended up burned on both sides."

"Alaska wasn't so bad," Michelle said. "Able and I took a very nice walk down to the lake."

"Minus the killers, Alaska was nice." Momma Peach raised her hand to her mouth and burped up some cayenne pepper. "Millie was supposed to make sure Mr. Sam went easy on the cayenne. Guess that didn't work out."

Michelle bit down on her lip and looked out into the wet night. A light was on in Max Moroz's trailer. "Mr. Moroz gave me the creeps from the first second I laid eyes on him. He reminded me of a mortician from a spooky movie."

"Oh, you and your horror movies," Momma Peach protested. "Don't plant images in my poor mind that I don't need. Oh, give me strength, give me strength."

Michelle kept staring out into the night. "I keep expecting to see zombie clowns walking around everywhere, too," she said in a low tone. "Something about this circus really gives me the creeps. I know zombies are not real and clowns are meant to entertain...but I can't help but feel that underneath it all lies something very sinister."

"Oh, give me strength," Momma Peach begged and threw her hand over her mouth. "You are going to cause me to have nightmares for the rest of my life."

"I'm sorry, Momma Peach, I can't help the way I feel." Michelle eyed Max's trailer and then spotted Officer Barnett walk by, bored, wet and irritated. "Barnett is not happy that I stuck him on night patrol."

Momma Peach spotted Officer Barnett. "Oh, you were a bit tough on the man. Let's face it, Vern Barnett is no Bruce Lee."

"I know, but, well," Michelle kicked at the ground, "I want my men fit and ready to brawl when the situation calls for it. Lately, I've noticed most of my guys putting on weight and getting really lazy. Sure, we don't live in a big city with lots of action on the streets, but that doesn't mean we can get out of practice. We've had three murders in our town this year."

"Each murder committed by an outsider."

"Maybe," Michelle agreed. "And that's my point. The outside world can and will invade our sleepy little town and my guys act like they're living in a perfect countryside utopia. Now, I like living in small-town Georgia just as much as the next guy, Momma Peach—and I wouldn't trade it for the world—but our town isn't a paradise. I mean, for crying out loud, look at Sam's little town. Who would have ever thought that his wife would blow it up?"

Michelle made a solid point that Momma Peach couldn't refute. "I know the good men and women wearing badges are a bit...complacent...but they are good folk."

"Deadly criminals don't care how good you are or aren't at heart, Momma Peach."

"Don't I know that as the truth," Momma Peach agreed.

"I'm going to create a physical fitness program and make my guys start working out some," Michelle said. "And I'm going to start making them take karate courses and hitting the range for target practice at least once a week. It's time for some tough love."

Momma Peach began to respond when she saw the door to Max's trailer open. Max popped his head out, looked up at the rain and then glanced around. He seemed satisfied, nodding his head before he ducked back inside. "Now what is that creepy snake up to?" Momma Peach wondered.

"He could be making sure the coast is clear. Barnett did just walk by."

Momma Peach nodded. "That's my guess. I bet you ten of my famous peach pies that Max Moroz will leave his trailer in the next minute or so and aim his old body toward poor Mr. Potter's trailer."

"Let's start counting."

Five minutes passed and then, to Michelle's shock, when the door to Max's trailer opened again, Lindsey Sung sprung out instead of Max. Lindsey hit the ground running and vanished into the dark rain before Michelle could say a single word. Her legs screamed at her to give chase, but her mind cautioned her to stand still. "Well, I'll be," Momma Peach said in a bothered voice, "it seems that Max Moroz is playing with Lindsey Sung, too."

Michelle narrowed her eyes and began thinking. It was clear that Lindsey didn't know she was around, which was good. If Lindsey knew Michelle was hiding in the main tent, the woman would have definitely attacked.

But what was Lindsey doing in Max's trailer? "Let's go speak to Max."

"Not yet," Momma Peach told Michelle. "If we go charging up, Max will know we were watching his hideout. Let's let some time pass and then I'll wander around some and pretend to be doing some late-night detective work, making sure that old man spots me."

Michelle knew Momma Peach made a good point. "Yeah, you're right, Momma Peach. And who knows, maybe Lindsey might come back, and we can trap her?"

"Let's hope," Momma Peach said and let out a silent fart. "Oh, Mr. Sam, what have you done to poor Momma Peach?"

Michelle backed away a few steps and fanned the air. "Oh, Momma Peach, aren't we in enough trouble as it is?" she begged.

Momma Peach pointed at her tush. "Baby, I can't control this end. She can barely control this end." Momma Peach pointed at her mouth. "Blame Mr. Sam and his blasted chili. Better yet, arrest Mr. Sam for making lethal chili. Lock him up and throw away the keys."

As Momma Peach fussed about Sam's chili, Max Moroz walked back to the couch in his trailer and sat down to think. Lindsey Sung had given him two choices: kill Momma Peach and live or die knowing someone else would kill her instead. Max wasn't in any mood to live as a guilty man, but he wasn't in any mood to die, either. "The woman must die, then," he whispered, "and I must find a new detective to capture me." Max leaned forward, picked up his milk jug, and took a few drinks of water. "Now, how am I going to kill that woman?" he asked himself. "I must be careful to leave a clue that will tell the new detective that all guilt points at me."

Max set down his milk jug, grabbed his cigar, stood up, and walked over to the tiny kitchen in his trailer. He opened a wooden drawer and withdrew a very sharp and deadly kitchen knife. "Ah yes," he said and raised the kitchen knife into the air and examined the blade, "this will do nicely. Now, I must lure that woman back into my trailer and complete my mission."

Max put the kitchen knife down, turned away from the kitchen area, and focused on his clown suits, arrayed in garish colors against the wall. "Which one should I wear?" he asked himself and grinned. "One last performance...and it will be my very best. And when the curtains fall, the world will know that Max Moroz was a man of talent, skill, and brilliance."

Outside in the rain, Lindsey Sung made her way back into the dark woods and began following the fence around toward the front of the fairgrounds. "Mr. Hayman, tonight you die," she whispered as the rain soaked her leather jacket. With those words, Lindsey vanished into the night.

CHAPTER SIX

*M*omma Peach began to hum a sweet old Christian hymn as she walked through the rain toward Lance Potter's trailer with her hands tucked behind her back. "Amazing Grace, how sweet the sound," she hummed, feeling confident that she was protected by a special and powerful love. "How sweet the sound...especially on a night like this," Momma Peach continued.

Michelle watched Momma Peach from the back entrance of the main tent, keeping a careful eye on Max Moroz's trailer. The light in the old man's trailer was still on but he had yet to show his face. Michelle wasn't sure how Lindsey Sung and Max Moroz were connected, but she did know that two spiders were more dangerous than one. However, Lindsey Sung was the more poisonous spider, Michelle thought, as her eyes watched Momma Peach walk through the rain. Sure, Max Moroz was a deadly killer, but his motive for murder was personal. Lindsey Sung killed without emotion or regret, conscience or concern for innocent life. Max Moroz's conscience appeared to be in a state of torment, pleading for silence and peace. Men like Max were like wounded dogs that could easily bite again and had to be taken seriously—and Michelle intended to take Max very seriously. Yet, her true concern was Lindsey Sung. The woman was a killer working for deadly men, and she had to be stopped. "Where did you go, Sung?" Michelle whispered to herself. "Are you going after Hayman? If you are, you might be in for a little surprise."

Momma Peach stopped walking, glanced over her shoulder at Max's trailer, and nodded. Knowing that her baby was watching her back gave her enough confidence to enter the mouth of madness on a rainy night. That's exactly how Momma Peach felt: as if she was willingly entering a lion's den, or the lair of a grizzly bear, except she knew she would find an insane, hideous clown ready to crawl out like a forbidden nightmare. "Oh, stop it," Momma Peach begged. "I don't need to see such spooky images in my mind. Now go back and sing about how sweet the grace of the Lord is."

As Momma Peach forced herself to begin humming again, Max Moroz slowly opened the door to his trailer, spotted Momma Peach standing in the rain, and grinned.

"It's a wet night, isn't it?" he called out in an accented voice that sent chills through Momma Peach.

Momma Peach turned around and spotted Max standing in the doorway to his trailer. She lifted her right hand and wiped rainwater away from her eyes. For a few seconds, she almost felt as if she were back in Sam's little desert town, caught in the dark storm, fighting for the truth against an unknown shadow. But then her mind cleared, and she focused on Max Moroz's murderous face. "I don't have time to be bothered, old man," she called out. "I still have to prove you killed poor Mr. Potter, rest his soul."

Max searched the rain, hoping Momma Peach's words didn't reach the annoying cops who were wandering back and forth through the circus. The coast was clear. There wasn't a cop in sight. "Perhaps a little tea on a rainy night?" he asked in a voice just loud enough to reach Momma Peach's ears. "A nice cup of hot tea and a little chat, yes?"

"What words do you want to put in my ears?" Momma Peach asked and carefully walked over to Max's trailer. "Old man, I ain't got time for games, no sir and no ma'am. I'm gonna bring you down and stuff you into the jailhouse, oh give me strength, yes sir and yes ma'am." Momma Peach pointed at Max. "You killed poor Mr. Potter and now I am gonna prove it, so don't waste my time playing games or I'll pop you so hard you'll hear bells from your old schooldays ringing in your head."

Max glanced around again. He didn't like Momma Peach mouthing off in an open area for prying ears to hear. "We need to talk," he said in a voice that came out stern and serious. "Our performance needs to be altered." Max swung his head back into his trailer and waited. Momma Peach glanced at the main tent, felt Michelle watching her, nodded, and walked into Max's trailer.

When she stepped inside, Max sat down on his couch. "Close the door."

Momma Peach closed the door, removed the hood from her head, straightened out the damp cloth covering her hair, and waited. Max picked up his cigar, took a puff, and sat very silent for a few minutes, leaving Momma Peach standing in confusion; or so he thought. "You gonna fix me some tea or what, old man?" Momma Peach finally asked, pretending to sound annoyed.

"In time," Max promised. "You can sit down if you wish."

"I will stand," Momma Peach said and let her eyes walk around the trailer. Max's vintage clown suit was laying over the small table. The sight of the suit conjured scary images of demented clowns chasing her through a house of broken mirrors. "Oh, give me strength," Momma Peach whispered.

Max saw Momma Peach set her eyes on his famous clown suit. "Do you like clowns?" he asked.

"I used to like clowns, now I'm not so fond of them

anymore." Momma Peach looked at Max. She wasn't sure which was worse: the face of a madman or the face of an insane clown? "What do you want to talk about?"

"I am a man of conscience," Max stated and puffed on his cigar, "and I have set you in motion to investigate my mind, yes?"

"So it seems."

Max nodded. "Perhaps I was too hasty, though?" Max suggested. "After all, even though I am a man of conscience, I am also a man of clear common sense." Max frowned. He didn't like back-pedaling on a mission. He wanted Momma Peach to discover the truth and set his conscience at ease. Now he would have to add more torment to his life and wait patiently for a second investigator to appear. Of course, he thought, the idea of a second murder did hold a strange and fascinating appeal to him. Murder, he mused, appeared to be a performance for the ages. Murder could be performed and remembered for many years to come, allowing him to once again stand in the main ring under the big tent with the spotlight on him alone. Yes, backpedaling was an unpleasant chore that set a sour taste in his chest—but then again, perhaps his conscience could endure punishment while he stepped into his costume and walked out into the ring again. "Do you have any family?" he asked Momma Peach.

Momma Peach looked into Max's creepy eyes. The old

man was beyond spooky to her. "I'm not here to talk about my personal life, old man." Momma Peach fought back a chill. In her mind, she saw a dark funeral home infested with a nest of deadly, hungry clowns with red glowing eyes. "Oh, stop it," she scolded herself.

Max took a puff of his cigar. "You seem...uncomfortable," he told Momma Peach. His eyes grinned.

"I ain't uncomfortable, old man. I am downright spooked. This here circus ain't right if you catch what I mean. This here circus is cursed. And you, old man, are part of the curse. You are a poison."

"Oh?" Max asked and put down his cigar. He slowly folded his arms together. "In the old days, when I performed in Russia, the nights were long and dark and the winters cruel and endless. Men's hearts were hungry for life and women were desperate for light. In those days," Max spoke in a low voice, his Russian accent growing rougher as the sight of a pale-lit circus shrouded in snowy fog and ice crystals appeared in his mind—a circus filled with dead men and forgotten women applauding mere shadows. He came out of his reverie and settled down into his seat. "Mister Max Moroz the Great Performer was a warm light in a dark world. I made the lifeless laugh and entertained meaningless minds...but the children," Max said, "the children mattered most."

"I doubt that," Momma Peach stated.

Max balled his hands into two tight fists and hit his couch. "The children matter!" he insisted. "The children mattered because I understood the dungeons they were locked in, in those little frozen villages and lifeless cities. I understood their nightmares. I understood their fears. I understood everything because I was once one of the lost children myself." Max's eyes grew dark with rage. "Little Max Moroz grew up in a cold, lifeless frozen orphanage, after all. His mother gave him a wonderful name, and then she died. In the orphanage, little Max Moroz was beaten with belts, hit with fists, smacked with hands, sent to bed starving and hurt...little Max Moroz endured thirteen years of nightmares before his escape." Max glared at Momma Peach. "Poor little Max Moroz was locked in a freezing basement, forced to walk over frozen ground in his bare feet, thrown into snow-covered work sheds and ordered to wash clothes in water with ice floating in it." Max held up his wrinkled hands. "Ever wash clothes in frozen water, lady, with your bare hands, in the middle of a Russian winter?"

"No," Momma Peach said, keeping her voice steady.

"Of course not," Max said and lowered his hands. He grew silent. When he did speak, the rage had left his voice. "Humor," Max finally said, "kept me alive. When I escaped, I worked with the little circuses that came and went. I would tell funny little anecdotes to distract my tormented mind. In time, a main character came to life...a clown. No more little Max, tormented and frozen. I was

Mister Max Moroz, the clown, the performer." Max looked into Momma Peach's eyes. "A simple clown who became little Max Moroz's teacher."

Momma Peach bit down on her lower lip. "Isn't it a bit late to complain about your childhood, old man?"

"Is it?" Max asked. "Perhaps the years have passed, lady, but the memories are still very much young and alive in my mind."

"Uh huh," Momma Peach said and deliberately rolled her eyes, "you're fishing for a bleeding heart and ain't gonna find one in me. You killed an innocent man and that ends the road of compassion, old man. I could care two rotten peaches what kind of childhood you had. All I care about is sending you to prison."

Max picked back up his cigar and took a puff. Yes, he thought, he was going to enjoy killing Momma Peach instead of letting the woman capture him. As a matter of fact, the more he stared at Momma Peach's scowling face, the more the thought of killing the woman excited him. "You speak dangerous words," he told Momma Peach. "You Americans pretend to own the world. You're all so arrogant, living in a fantasy world in which you deem yourselves kings and queens while innocent people suffer in other parts of the world." Max tapped his cigar on his knee. "You know no sacrifice, no honor, no bravery. No suffering. You are overstuffed pigs feeding off the spoils of the poor, living in filthy pride that someday will be destroyed."

"Listen, punk," Momma Peach snapped and pointed a hard finger at Max, "many—and I mean many—good men and women have died to make America free. Sure, America might take a turn downhill toward a pile of manure once in a while, maybe more often than we'd like, but that doesn't mean we disrespect what America stands for. Men stormed Normandy beach and fought the enemy mighty brave...men marched out to fight for independence against the British, cold and hungry...men sweated in the hot jungles of Vietnam and shivered in the frozen winters that soak Korea. So don't you ever, and I mean ever, insult their memory and tell me we don't know honor or bravery, you punk!"

Max tapped his cigar on his knee again. Momma Peach's eyes told him to stand down. It was time to switch gears. There was no sense in venting his displeasure over a country that was not his own. His personal opinion of America was on mute. He needed to focus on his victim and begin setting the stage for his performance—a forced performance, perhaps, but a performance nonetheless. So what if Lindsey Sung had threatened his life? The woman, without realizing it, had actually renewed his crumbling spirit of performance. "I left a clue for you," he spoke in a cold tone. "The clue will be revealed tomorrow night at midnight. Come back to the circus...alone. When you arrive, come to my trailer, lady, and you will receive more instructions."

"I ain't in the mood for games."

"Neither am I," Max said. He put down his cigar, reached under the couch, and pulled out a gun. "Here, catch," he said and tossed the gun at Momma Peach. Momma Peach caught the gun on instinct, then realized her mistake and threw the gun down onto the floor. "Very good," Max said and pulled out a second gun from underneath the couch and aimed it at Momma Peach. "Now I have your fingerprints on a murder weapon. Now," he added with a sinister grin, "you will do as I say. Return tomorrow night at midnight or face a very harsh penalty, lady."

"You're one sick potato," Momma Peach growled at Max. "I'm gonna tear you a new one but right, yes sir and yes ma'am. I am gonna tan your hide from here to the Mississippi River! Oh, give me strength."

"Get out of my trailer...for now at least," Max hissed at Momma Peach. "Return at midnight, alone. No cops. If you fail my orders, you will—"

"Yeah, yeah, suffer a harsh penalty. You ain't saying nothing I haven't heard before, you rotten hack." Momma Peach kicked the gun on the floor at Max. "I will be back at midnight with my thinking cap on."

"Perhaps," Max said and pointed at the door with his gun. "Leave."

"Before I do," Momma Peach said, "tell me one thing."

"The hour is late, lady."

"Oh, who cares," Momma Peach snapped. "All I want to know is why you went off your medicine," Momma Peach said and stormed back outside into the rain, leaving Max sitting alone on his couch.

"Well?" Michelle asked as soon as Momma Peach returned to the main tent.

"That old Russian is crazier than a cat trapped in a room full of rocking chairs," Momma Peach sighed. "Baby, Max Moroz is planning something really bad...either he's gonna kill me or frame me or make me kill someone else."

"What do you mean?" Michelle asked.

Momma Peach explained about the gun Max tossed at her. "My fingerprints are all over that gun now. That old skunk caught me off guard. Oh, I could piledrive that old man straight back to Old Mother Russia."

Michelle bit down on her lower lip. "Momma Peach, let's go back to the station. I don't think Lindsey Sung will return tonight, and Max Moroz isn't going anywhere. My guys will watch the grounds...I hope," Michelle said and wrapped her arm around Momma Peach. "Let's go get some coffee."

Momma Peach looked into Michelle's face and nodded. "I could use a cup of coffee," she said and let out a fart. "Mr. Sam, I am gonna piledrive you next, if my stomach survives the night, that is!"

Lindsey Sung crouched down behind a parked cruiser and studied the sleepy police station. The station looked tired, old and worn-down; it weathered the hard rain like an old man wondering if he was going to catch pneumonia or not. Inside the station, Lindsey assumed, were a few police officers pulling the night shift, probably sitting around drinking coffee and eating donuts and getting fat. Killing off a few lazy cops wouldn't be a problem. Doing so unnoticed would require careful planning and perfect timing. Because Michelle's car was nowhere in sight, Lindsey knew she had time to spare and didn't rush her thoughts. She wanted to extract Lionel Hayman without any complication. When she heard the back door to the police station open, she focused her attention on a tall, thin man in his early fifties who stepped outside and jogged over to a police car. He sat a minute in the cruiser and then drove away. "Perfect," Lindsey grinned and slunk over to the back door. "Perfect."

The sound of an approaching car caused Lindsey to run back behind the police car she had been hiding behind and crouch down. Michelle pulled up into the back parking lot of the station, parked in her usual spot, and exited her car with Momma Peach. Lindsey watched her hurry over to the back door, unlock it with a special key, and step inside with Momma Peach close behind. The sight of Michelle and Momma Peach caused her concern. The two women were obviously on duty and had come from some location, possibly the circus, which meant they might have spotted her leaving Max Moroz's trailer. If that were the case, Lindsey knew she would have to return and kill Max instead of allowing Max the opportunity to kill Momma Peach. "You two were supposed to be away for the night," she hissed. "Where have you been?"

Lindsey felt anger and fury grip her heart as her patience began to melt away. How had a simple stop in a small, hick town caused so many problems for her? She had managed to run the black market drugs right under the noses of the FBI, CIA and DEA. Now she was crouched behind an old cruiser, drenched in rain, trying to figure out how to extract Lionel Hayman from a run-down police station. Furthermore, the building was infested with Momma Peach and Michelle Chan. "You'll pay," Lindsey hissed at Michelle and looked out into the pouring rain. "Your friend will pay...Max Moroz will pay...they will all pay."

Lindsey closed her eyes, took a deep breath, and, on stealthy legs, ran away from the police station, jogged down a wet street, and began making her way toward town. When she reached the main street where Momma Peach's bakery was located, Lindsey simply walked up to the front display window of the bakery, removed a dagger strapped around her left arm, and jammed the hilt of the knife into the window. The window exploded and crashed down onto the sidewalk. A loud alarm erupted and began wailing up and down the street like a confused Paul Revere. "That should bring them to me. I will kill them both here and draw all the police to this location, and then go back for Mr. Hayman," she said as she walked away from the broken window and maneuvered around the back of the bakery into the alley.

As Lindsey hid in the back alley, Michelle took a sip of coffee. "Not bad," she told Momma Peach in a sleepy voice. But her brief peace was interrupted when a female officer in her late fifties stuck her head into the office with a look of concern on her face. "Detective, Momma Peach. Dispatch just received a call." The woman looked at Momma Peach with apologetic eyes. "Someone broke the front window out of your bakery, Momma Peach."

"Lindsey Sung," Michelle said and sprung to her feet.

Momma Peach, surprisingly, remained seated. Her feet were tired. Her head was wet. Her tummy was upset. She didn't feel like racing off into the rainy night again. "Sit back down."

"Why?" Michelle asked.

136

Momma Peach took a sip of hot coffee from a brown mug. "Why would Lindsey Sung break my window?"

"Detective, I sent Fred Chert down to Momma Peach's bakery," the woman told Michelle. "Should I dispatch anyone else? Maybe Milton?"

"Not yet, Joan," Michelle said, staring into Momma Peach's eyes. "Let's see what Fred comes up with, okay?"

"Sure thing," the woman said and closed the office door and went back to her station, leaving Michelle and Momma Peach alone.

"A trap?" Michelle asked.

Momma Peach nodded. "Yes, a trap. My mind might feel like mush right now and my stomach may have stunk up your car pretty bad, but I still has my smarts intact." Momma Peach took another sip of coffee. "That Lindsey thinks Lionel Hayman is locked in this here police station, right?"

"Yes."

"If you wanted to break someone out...or even kill someone...what would you do?" Momma Peach asked. "What would you do if you had too many flies spoiling your nice, murder-filled picnic?"

Michelle considered Momma Peach's question. "I would use a jar of honey to draw the flies away, Momma Peach."

"Exactly," Momma Peach replied and grew silent. "That awful woman breaks my window, we come running, she kills us...every cop in town runs to the scene, leaving this here police station practically empty, and then she attacks again."

Michelle rubbed her face. "You're right on track tonight, Momma Peach. But that doesn't mean I can just sit here and do nothing. If Lindsey Sung is lingering around your bakery I need to go and find her. I can't hide and wait for her to spring another trap. I'm a cop, Momma Peach."

"And a smart cop to boot," Momma Peach added, "which means, right now you need to be using those smarts to out-think a very deadly enemy."

Michelle snatched up her coffee and took a drink. "We need to draw Lindsey Sung to the station, is that what you're trying to say to me?" she asked.

"Maybe," Momma Peach asked, "or maybe we need to draw Lindsey Sung someplace else altogether." Momma Peach leaned back in her chair and began to think and let the sound of falling rain calm her mind. After a few minutes, she spoke: "Send a message to Officer Chert."

"A message?" Michelle asked.

"Tell him you're transferring Mr. Lionel Hayman to a different location and to keep Momma Peach's bakery under lockdown. If Lindsey Sung is hiding in the rain, maybe she might hear the message—"

"So she'll come running back to the station. Brilliant, Momma Peach," Michelle said in a calm voice.

"We can only hope," Momma Peach told Michelle. "Otherwise all we can do is sit here with our thinking caps on while that black widow sits out in the rain hatching more plans."

Michelle stood up. "I'll talk with Joan and have her send the message over to Fred Chert." Michelle hurried over to her office door, opened it, and then stepped back. "Sam...Millie, what are you doing here?"

Sam walked into Michelle's office and pointed at Momma Peach. "You were supposed to be at home. Old Joe called me. He was worried."

Momma Peach watched Sam shake rainwater off his brown leather coat. He had on his cowboy hat and looked handsome and rugged. Millie stood by his side like a loving wife, wearing a simple gray rain jacket that reminded Momma Peach just how humble the woman really was. "Mr. Sam, I had business—"

"Not if that business risks your life," Sam told Momma Peach in an upset voice. "We're a family, Momma Peach. If Old Joe was worried, well, that tells me a lot." Sam took off his hat. "Momma Peach, you told me you were going home after supper. Why did you lie to me? Why didn't you at least call and let someone know?"

"It's Lindsey Sung," Michelle told Sam and closed her

office door and looked at Sam with worried eyes. "Sam, Momma Peach was only trying to protect you. She lied to me, too."

"I didn't lie," Momma Peach objected. "I simply told everyone that spending a restful night at home seemed mighty nice."

"You led us to believe—" Sam began.

"I simply changed my mind," Momma Peach enforced her statement. "This Lindsey Sung gal is deadlier than a diseased tick on a sick dog. I don't want Mr. Sam tangling with her. I love you and know you're awful brave, but Lindsey Sung will kill you if you tangles with her."

Millie nodded. "That's what I've been telling Sam all night," she explained. Millie gave Sam a concerned look. "Sam, Lindsey Sung is a vicious woman."

"I'm not even sure I can defeat her," Michelle told Sam and plopped down on the corner of her desk and folded her arms. "Sam, I'm being honest. If...and when...I go toe-to-toe with Lindsey Sung, the woman might kill me."

Sam stared at Michelle. He couldn't believe his eyes or ears. Was Michelle actually showing fear? As far as he knew, the young woman he considered as close as a daughter could kick anyone's backside, including his. "Hey," he said and put his hand on Michelle's shoulder, "surely this woman can't—"

"She is a killer," Michelle said and raised her eyes up to Sam's face. "Sam, I'm not backing down from the fight, but I'm also not sure I will walk away alive." Michelle drew in a deep breath. "Lindsey Sung just broke out the front window to Momma Peach's bakery...or so we believe."

"What?" Sam exclaimed. He spun around and focused on Momma Peach. "Momma Peach, what is going on? Never mind that...where have you been all night?"

"At the circus messing with a very sick clown," Momma Peach told Sam. "And now there's another sick clown hanging round my bakery." Momma Peach bit down on her lower lip and explained why she thought Lindsey Sung broke the front display window. "Michelle was just going to send a message to Officer Chert when you two appeared and—" Momma Peach let out a horrible fart. "Oh dear, excuse me..."

Millie blushed and stepped back. Sam shook his head. "My chili?"

"You better believe your chili is turning my tummy into a rumbling volcano," Momma Peach fussed. "Mr. Sam, I like cayenne pepper just as much as the next person, but you...oh you...you drink it like it's winter eggnog!"

"I'll go have Joan send the message," Michelle said in a quick voice and hurried out of her office, leaving Sam and Millie to face Momma Peach.

Millie reached into the pocket of her jacket and pulled out a bottle of Pepto Bismol. "Here, Momma Peach, have some. My stomach has been upset tonight, too." Millie frowned at Sam. "It was a little too heavy on the cayenne...I didn't want to hurt your feelings after all you've done for Lidia and me today."

"No offense taken," Sam told Millie and patted his own stomach. "I didn't tell anyone, but I accidentally spilled the bottle of cayenne pepper into my chili tonight. Sorry guys."

"You spilled a whole bottle of cayenne pepper into your famous chili and still served a bowl to me?" Momma Peach asked Sam. "Oh, give me strength, give me strength, you are trying to finish me off before it's my time."

Sam rubbed the back of his neck with his left hand and watched Millie hand the Pepto Bismol to Momma Peach. "Look on the bright side, Momma Peach...cayenne pepper is really good for your heart."

Momma Peach chugged the bottle of Pepto Bismol and gave Sam a hard eye. "Remind me to cook supper for you next week Mr. Sam," she said through gritted teeth. "I know how to use cayenne pepper, too."

Sam winced and stepped back. "Well...uh, the elephant is settled in at least. And Lidia, she ended up coming back to the farm and insisted she be allowed to sleep close to Melanie."

"Lidia loves her elephant," Millie sighed. "I offered to let her sleep in my RV, but she insisted on being near Melanie."

Momma Peach finished off the bottle of Pepto Bismol. "Melanie is a sweet elephant that needs her momma," Momma Peach said and let out a little burp. "Mr. Sam, Ms. Millie, I sure am tired and want to go home, but I have a feeling this night is far from over. So since you two are here and—"

Old Joe popped his head into the office. "Hey, Momma Peach," he said in a careful voice, "you okay?" Old Joe looked at Sam. "Sorry, Mr. Sam. I couldn't wait in your truck another second."

"You brought that old alley cat with you, Mr. Sam?" Momma Peach asked.

"He was worried, Momma Peach." Sam motioned for Old Joe to enter the office.

Old Joe walked into the office and looked at Momma Peach. "I know you don't think too much of me, Momma Peach, but when you didn't come home, I got mighty worried. So please don't be mad at me for calling Mr. Sam and his new friend."

Momma Peach saw a tender care running back and forth

in Old Joe's eyes. The man had been sincerely worried about her. "Oh, I ain't mad at you, Old Joe. I am plum worn down to the bone, but I ain't mad. As a matter of fact, I'm grateful you cared enough to even be worried."

Old Joe shrugged his shoulders. "Ain't nobody in the world caring for me like you're doing...and well, I am grateful...and mighty sorry I tried to make Ms. Kung Fu give me money earlier for picking the safe."

"Picking a safe?" Sam asked. He looked at Momma Peach with confused eyes. "Momma Peach, what in the world is going on here? What have you and Old Joe been up to? What is going on out there at that circus?"

Momma Peach pointed at the office window. "Mr. Sam, out there in that rain are two spooky clowns that mean business," she said. "Lindsey Sung and Max Moroz. Yes sir and yes ma'am, out there in that rain are two deadly clowns...one who wants to get back into the spotlight and the other trying to stay out of the spotlight. What a mess, what a peachy mess."

Outside in the rain, Lindsey Sung listened to the wail of the alarm and watched from around the corner as police lights flashed in the darkness, certain that Michelle and Momma Peach were about to arrive.

CHAPTER SEVEN

*L*indsey Sung slipped around the side of Momma Peach's bakery and saw a cop standing half in and half out of his patrol car speaking to his radio. "Yeah, Joan, I got it. I'll wrap up business here and get back to the station and help transfer that fella Hayman to his new location...yeah, no sight of the vandal. Probably the Winston boys again. They're always causing trouble...yeah, I'll go out and talk to their folks tomorrow... okay, see you in a bit."

"So that's your game," Lindsey hissed, watching Officer Chert walk over to the broken display window and kick at some broken glass. She felt rage erupt in her heart. Instead of luring her prey to the bakery, they used her scheme against her in order to relocate Lionel Hayman to a new location, thinking they could do it without her knowledge. "You're a clever one, Chan." Lindsey stood silent and let the rain fall on her and then she acted. She left her hidden position and walked straight up to Fred Chert with her hands out in front of her. "I broke the window," she said with mock remorse.

Officer Chert jerked his head to the side and spotted Lindsey. He scrambled backward, went for his gun, and nearly tripped over his own feet. "Stay right there!" he shouted.

"I'm surrendering peacefully," Lindsey promised in a sickeningly sweet tone. "I know it was wrong of me to break the window. I was upset."

Officer Chert stared through the falling rain at Lindsey. The woman sure was beautiful, he thought. But he had been warned to be cautious of Lindsey Sung and to use extra security measures at all times. "Just keep your hands where I can see them."

"I will," Lindsey promised, pretending to act innocent and contrite. "I'm sorry I broke the window, officer. I know it was wrong of me. But I just got so mad at my boyfriend that I...well, I took my anger out on a window."

"Aren't you Lindsey Sung, the woman who works with the circus?" Officer Chert asked.

"I used to work with the circus. Mr. Hayman was arrested, which means I don't have a job anymore. I called my boyfriend and asked for help, but he told me to take a hike," Lindsey lied. "Oh, he made me so mad."

Lindsey allowed her rage to bubble quietly to the surface, just enough to make tears fall from her eyes. "I don't know what I'm going to do," she choked back a fake sob. "The circus was my life and now I'm stranded with only a few dollars to my name."

Officer Chert stared at Lindsey. His gut told him to be careful, but his mind urged him to play hero for the damsel in distress. "Now, now," he said and lowered his gun, "we all make mistakes. It was wrong of you to break this window, but we all lose our temper at times. At least you had enough integrity to admit your mistake."

Lindsey wiped at her eyes. "Are you taking me to jail?"

"I'm afraid I might have to," Officer Chert told Lindsey.

"Oh dear," Lindsey burst out into tears, "what am I going to do?"

Officer Chert placed his gun back in the holster hooked to the utility belt around his waist and walked up to Lindsey, gently reaching out his hand to touch her shoulder. As soon as he did, Lindsey narrowed her eyes and laid the man out cold with one single punch.

Officer Chert crashed down onto the wet sidewalk and collapsed without knowing what hit him. "Never fails. Better to let the mongrels come to you," she grinned and quickly worked to stuff Officer Chert's body into the truck of his patrol car. When the task was complete, she jumped into the front seat and drove back to the police station.

Inside the police station, Michelle was talking with Lionel Hayman in the interrogation room. Momma Peach was sitting behind the one-way mirror listening. "You know Lindsey Sung is going to kill you," Michelle said, leaning her foot on a metal chair and taking a sip of hot coffee.

Lionel Hayman stared up at Michelle with his hands cuffed in front of him. He was terrified. If Lindsey Sung didn't kill him, the men she was working for would send someone else to finish the job. Lindsey Sung was small potatoes compared to trained killers backed by a very powerful payroll. Could speaking to a cop save his life? Could he try and make a deal that would somehow give him enough leverage to escape his enemies? He needed someone more powerful than this small-town nobody sitting across the table from him. "I want to speak with the FBI."

"You talk with me first, pal," Michelle warned Lionel. "Lindsey Sung is loose. I'm the only cop around that can save your hide. Start talking and no lies. I've gone through the files. I know about the black market drug operation you've been running under the big tent."

Lionel shifted in his seat. The metal chair was uncomfortable. "Detective," he spoke in his cultured English accent, "the men I work for can kill us both in a matter of hours. The business you refer to is merely a small operation compared to the major markets operating right here in your country. My area of expertise—"

"The cancer medicine."

"Yes," Lionel acknowledged. "It isn't dangerous. I am not a monster. I sell life-saving medicine to the highest bidder. And before you lecture me, Detective, please save your breath. The pharmaceutical companies have the cure to cancer, they simply refuse to let the common people in on their little secret. The real monsters sit on gold thrones making billions off of the suffering of innocent people." Lionel shook his head. "Chemotherapy is a very profitable business compared to a single cure for cancer."

"You can't be serious. What proof do you have?"

"Are you really that blind, Detective?" Lionel huffed. "You have eyes to see. You see the GMO crops that are grown, the poison chemicals made into processed foods, the numbing of the American mindset." Lionel tapped the table with his cuffed hand. "Your precious free market economy is simply the tool of corporate America, which controls all your grocery stores and fills them with cancerous foods." Lionel stared at Michelle as if the woman was stupid. "Hospitals and pharmacies are nothing more than dope centers, designed to numb the same cancers and diseases caused by corporate America. They sell you the disease, and then they sell you the cure.

Every corner store sells booze and cancerous cigarettes, sure, but mainly they sell you those lovely wonderful fattening processed snacks, those sugar-filled sodas and energy drinks. There are fast food restaurants as far as the eye can see, filled with cancerous foods, deliberately designed that way, I might add. Your precious corporate America works hand in hand with the pharmaceutical companies to poison brain-dead people who do not have enough sense to see that they are being programmed and murdered by the very drinks they reach for every day. The medications I sell may be for cancer, but for those in the know, these medicines also optimize life, they strengthen the body and empower the mind." His eyes glowed a little with grim satisfaction. "So is it wrong to sell this life-saving medicine to those who are awake? To people who care about life rather than finding the next processed cheeseburger to shove down their throats?"

Michelle felt sick listening to his diseased logic. "You're not a saint, Mr. Hayman. You're in this for the money. Don't try to sell me a sob story."

Lionel tapped the table again. "I once suffered from cancer, Detective, and nearly died. My brother spent a fortune to save my life. In return, I decided to show my gratitude by working for the people who allowed him to purchase the cancer medicine I needed." Lionel stared at Michelle. "I understood the risk. I knew the dangers. It's true that I am scared for my life and that I know my days are numbered..." Lionel stopped talking.

Michelle sipped her coffee. "Did you kill Lance Potter?"

"Of course not," Lionel exclaimed.

"You planted the whiskey bottle in his trailer, didn't you?"

"Yes," Lionel confessed. "That was all Lindsey's idea."

"Did Lindsey kill Lance Potter?"

"No," Lionel answered truthfully. He looked up at Michelle. "Lindsey did kill Greenson. I...asked her to spare the man's life, but she insisted that the man's death was the only thing that could free us from this miserable town. She devised a clever scheme and we were confident it would work." Lionel looked down at his hands. "My attorney was the cherry on the cake, as they say...unfortunately, you got in the way, and then my attorney turned coward on me and fled for his life. Detective, I'm not a killer. It's true that I'm a man who has...made difficult choices, but I'm not a killer."

"You knew Lindsey Sung was planning to kill Mr. Greenson and that she killed him, and you said nothing. That makes you an accessory to murder," Michelle informed Lionel. "An honest man would not allow an innocent man to die in order to open an escape hatch." Michelle set down the brown mug she was holding. "You chose a very hard path for yourself, Mr. Hayman."

Lionel raised his eyes. "Fear makes a man act foolishly,

Detective. I'm very much afraid of Ms. Sung. Perhaps it was wrong to remain silent, but you must understand, I have orders to carry out, on pain of death. The men I work for are remorseless, soulless." Lionel settled his body into a suitable position. "My brother was a decent lad, Detective. But sadly, he always seemed to find companions among the wrong type of people. When I said that he paid a fortune for my cancer medicine, I wasn't exaggerating. You see, my brother signed a lifelong contract to repay that debt...when he died, the contract fell into my lap. I had no choice but to show my gratitude or pay the debt with my life. Do you really think a man of my stature would choose to own a foul, low-life circus?" Lionel gave Michelle a strange look.

"Ah," Michelle said, "your employees at the circus are working for the black market gang too, right?"

"Not all of them...only a select handful," Lionel confessed. "The circus travels where it is ordered to travel. At times, certain people are dismissed and certain people are hired on...and at times...the men I work for send me people."

Michelle sat down. She looked at the two-way mirror. "Mr. Hayman, I admit that I couldn't care less what happens to the likes of you, but with that said, maybe we can make a deal with each other."

"A deal?" Lionel asked. "Come now detective, do you really think you can destroy the men I work for? These men have their hands in the pockets of some very powerful senators, don't forget. I'm sure you saw that in the paperwork you stole from me. The best you will be able to accomplish is closing down the circus. The men I work for will simply slap your annoying hand away and create another undercover operation and continue on without skipping a beat. Why? Because your FBI, CIA, DEA, all of your so-called alphabet-soup agencies are bought and paid for, controlled by politicians who create wars for profit and use politics to keep the people divided. The politicians depend on the black market just as much as the criminals do."

Michelle knew Lionel was speaking the truth. She bit down on her lower lip. "Okay, Mr. Hayman, right now I want to focus on the murders of Mr. Potter and Mr. Greenson. I won't concern myself with the black market trade in cancer medicines. As much as it hurts me to agree with you, I admit that you are right. I can see that now. I was hoping you might give me some names, but that hope was made in vain—"

"Well, that's partially right," Lionel interrupted. "You must realize, Detective, that there is a constant civil war taking place among these agencies—a constant war for power in which certain victories and losses are being traded back and forth. Within your own FBI, there is a war taking place. If...perhaps...I play my cards right, I might be able to make a deal with some people who might find me of some use. You see, not everyone is content with the men I work for." Lionel stared at Michelle. "The profits I make are used to fund politicians who my bosses support. It's a vicious, ugly cycle, Detective, in which many weapons are used, including medicine. But why should you bother yourself when you can watch programmed television that tells you what to think?"

Michelle picked up her coffee and took a sip. She wasn't in the mood to be lectured on how the American public was willfully surrendering to a group of evil men. She wanted to focus on her job. "You said that Lindsey Sung killed Mr. Greenson. Will you testify to that in a court of law?"

"What's in the deal for me?" Lionel asked.

"If you testify in a court of law—"

"If I testify in a court of law, I will insist that I acted out of fear for my own life, which I did," Lionel interrupted Michelle. "In return, I will insist that I be placed in the Witness Protection Program. Are we clear, Detective?"

"Fair enough," Michelle said. "But listen to me, Lindsey Sung is loose and she is bound to kill you, Mr. Hayman. You are a threat to her employers. Your best shot of surviving until morning is cooperating with me, okay?"

"Of course," Lionel agreed. "Detective, I'm not a foolish man. My chances of surviving are very narrow, even if I do make it into a court of law. There is no reasonable point to object to your duty any longer. If I dared to escape, where would I run to? I would be tracked down and killed within days. My only chance is to play on the minds of the men who are at war with my employers."

Michelle nodded and stood up. "Sit tight, Mr. Hayman. I'll have someone walk you back to your cell in a few minutes." Michelle left the interrogation room and met Momma Peach out in the hallway. "Well?" she asked.

Momma Peach chewed on a piece of peppermint. "Hide that skunk away and make sure his look-alike is sitting in his cell," Momma Peach told Michelle in a thoughtful voice. "It was clever of you to find Mr. Dillard and ask him to play along."

"Mr. Dillard is on probation and attending his AA meetings on a regular basis. He was happy to help me because I drive him to his meetings sometimes. I doubt he'll ever drive drunk again."

"Let's pray not," Momma Peach said. "Do you think Lindsey Sung will come here?"

Before Michelle could answer, Joan came hurrying down the hallway with a worried expression on her face. "Detective, I haven't been able to get in touch with Fred. I relayed your message to him, but I forgot to tell him your message was a decoy. All I'm getting from him is static."

"I guess that answers your question, Momma Peach," Michelle said in a quick voice. "Joan, take Mr. Hayman back down to the basement and lock him in the old cell. Station someone down there to guard him. Then check on Mr. Dillard. If he's sleeping, wake him up."

Joan nodded and hurried away to carry out her duties. Michelle turned to Momma Peach with a grim look. "I gave Mr. Dillard a gun, Momma Peach. If Lindsey gets past our defenses, then our last hope of stopping her will be Mr. Dillard."

Momma Peach looked into Michelle's face. Her baby was worried and so was she.

Lindsey pulled up to the side of the police station. She stared at the station with careful eyes. Somewhere inside the station house, Lionel Hayman was being protected by weak cops—and somewhere inside the station house was her mortal enemy. "Let's be very smart," Lindsey whispered and called the station. "Let me speak to Detective Chan," she ordered.

"Who is calling?" Joan asked.

"Lindsey Sung."

"Oh..." Joan said and connected the call to Michelle's office.

Michelle picked up on the second ring. "Detective Chan—"

"Listen closely to me, cop. If you want to see Officer Chert alive again, you will release Lionel Hayman to me within the next hour, do I make myself clear?" Lindsey hissed.

Michelle waved at Momma Peach, Sam, Millie and Old Joe and asked them to stop talking. "I'm listening, Sung."

"I could have walked into your drab station, Chan, and killed you all. You were smart not to fall for my trick at the bakery. Now I'm tired of the games. I want Hayman. If you cooperate, I will let you and your pathetic friends live," Lindsey lied. She kicked herself for trying a pointless trick against an experienced cop. "I should have attacked first instead of attempting to trick you. Fool me once... However, if you do as I say, I will back down."

"No, you won't," Michelle told Lindsey. "You'll never back down because you want us all dead. I don't negotiate with criminals. You're going to have to come inside and try to take Mr. Hayman by force, Sung. We'll be waiting for you."

"I'll kill your cop, Chert!" Lindsey exploded.

Michelle squeezed the phone. Lindsey would surely kill Fred, assuming the man wasn't dead already. But she couldn't walk into a trap. She looked at Momma Peach with desperate eyes. "She has Fred, Momma Peach, and is threatening to kill him unless I release Hayman to her."

Momma Peach nodded. "So let's give her that old skunk," she said in a calm voice.

"Okay, Sung, let's make a deal...Hayman for Chert," Michelle spoke into the phone with a sick feeling in her gut.

"Call your worthless dogs away from the circus and meet me there in one hour. If I see a cop around, it's the end of the line for the mutt Chert in my trunk. Bring Hayman and no one else, I'm warning you! Tell you what...bring that overstuffed woman you travel with, if it makes you feel better. If I see anyone else, Chan, I'll make sure Chert suffers before I kill him."

"I'll be there," Michelle promised. "And when I arrive, we'll finish our fight, Sung."

"I'm counting on it," Lindsey grinned, ended the call, and drove away.

Michelle put down the phone. "Momma Peach, it looks like you and me are going back to the circus tonight."

"Not alone," Sam told Michelle.

"Alone," Michelle replied. "Sam, if Sung sees anyone other than Momma Peach and myself she'll kill Officer Chert. We don't have a choice."

"Oh, maybe we do," Momma Peach told Michelle. "We have Mr. Dillard. I could kiss you all over your forehead for being so clever." Momma Peach looked at Sam.

"You're going to have to sit tight right here with Old Joe and Millie."

"No," Sam objected. "Momma Peach, we're a family. Families stick together."

"But I am also a cop," Michelle told Sam. "And right now, the life of another cop is in danger, Sam, and that comes first. I can't risk you coming with us. I have to think about Fred Chert's life. I know you can understand that."

Sam threw his hand to the back of his neck and rubbed it in frustration. "Yeah, I understand," he said, feeling helpless. "This is one of those times when I wish I didn't."

Millie reached out and took Sam's hand. "It'll be okay, Sam. Right now, we all just need to have a little faith."

Sam looked into Millie's caring eyes. The woman calmed his upset heart. "I don't like sitting on the back burner when people I love are in danger, Millie."

"I can see that," Millie promised.

Sam looked at Michelle and then to Momma Peach. "If anything happens to you two I'll never forgive myself."

"If Lindsey Sung sees you, Sam, she'll kill an innocent man," Michelle said. She bent down and checked her gun. "Okay, Momma Peach, let's go."

Momma Peach nodded, smiled at Sam and then pointed at Old Joe. "Old Joe, make sure Mr. Sam sits tight. I know he's a real cowboy and might try to head out on the range as soon as I leave." Old Joe nodded. Sam looked down at the floor.

Michelle picked up the phone on her desk. "Joan, call the guys back from the fairgrounds, and in thirty minutes I want you to drive Mr. Dillard out to the circus. Only you, okay?"

"Okay," Joan agreed.

"And make sure Mr. Hayman stays heavily guarded," Michelle said and put down the phone. "Let's go, Momma Peach." Momma Peach followed Michelle out of the office and closed the office door behind her. She walked out into the rainy night with Michelle, got her short little legs moving across the parking lot, and crawled into the front seat of a damp car. "Sung is up to something," Michelle told Momma Peach.

"She sure is," Momma Peach agreed. "She is going to try and kill four birds with one stone." Momma Peach buckled her seatbelt and sat back in her seat as Michelle got the car moving through the rain and drove down a dark, wet street past sleepy houses and saturated lawns. Momma Peach let her eyes fall on the houses. Some houses had lights on, others didn't. Each house seemed inviting, warm and welcoming. She felt her insides longing to be inside a warm kitchen sipping hot coffee and eating a slice of peach pie. "When this is all over, remind me that I want some peach pie."

"Okay, Momma Peach," Michelle said, driving through back neighborhoods, deliberately avoiding the main roads. The homes made her yearn for family and peace, too. "Momma Peach, if...something happens to me tonight, tell Able...that he means..." Michelle stopped talking. Tears began to fall from her eyes.

Momma Peach looked over at her baby. "Oh, baby," she said and wiped Michelle's tears away.

Michelle pulled over to the side of the road and looked at Momma Peach with scared eyes. "Momma Peach, I'm not sure that I can defeat Sung. Sung is way different from an oversized trucker in a pool hall or some idiot bikers in a bus station. I'll fight her, but...if she kills me...just know I love you very...oh, so very much." Michelle reached out and hugged Momma Peach with all of her might. "Oh Momma Peach, you're my heart...you're my real Momma and I love you so much," Michelle cried.

Momma Peach pulled Michelle into her loving arms and held her. "I love you even more," she whispered as tears started to fall from her eyes. "I love you more than words can say. You live in a very special place inside of my heart that no one can touch."

Michelle leaned up. "If I do die tonight," she whispered, "I'll die knowing that you loved me and that's enough."

"Oh, don't break my heart," Momma Peach begged. "I ain't gonna let nothing happen to you, do you hear? I am meaner than a pebble boiling in a pot of black-eyed peas. Lindsey Sung is in for a fight she ain't ready for, because no one makes my Michelle cry and gets away with it, no sir and no ma'am!"

"Your hands will be full with Max Moroz. I think we both know Lindsey Sung is going to the circus because she is going to set him up to kill you."

"Assuming he does and she kills you, then she'll kill that old man and Mr. Hayman...four lives with one stone," Momma Peach agreed. "That woman is clever, but so are we." Momma Peach wiped at Michelle's tears. "My momma didn't raise no fool. I know that we're about to walk into the den of lions, but I sure ain't afraid."

Michelle found strength and comfort in Momma Peach's words. "You make me feel good, Momma Peach," she said and drew in a deep breath. "I...I'm a cop and I'll die a cop if that's what I have to do tonight. But oh, Momma Peach, I do want to be a mother someday. Tonight I kept thinking...what if I had a baby...and Sung was after me...and went after my baby...maybe the time has come for me to finally set my badge down?"

Momma Peach understood Michelle's fear. Her mind began to wonder many what-ifs. What if Michelle and Able did have a baby? What if a criminal went after their child? What if Michelle was killed? The what-ifs began to torment her mind. Losing her own husband had been horrible enough—and losing Michelle would destroy her.

Lindsey Sung sure was doing a good job of placing a heavy shadow over her heart. "The time will come when you will know when it's right to either continue being a cop or...quit the force."

"Being a cop is who I am," Michelle confessed. "I couldn't imagine not being a cop, Momma Peach. But...when I become a mother...my baby will have to come first. I...know I sound paranoid and spooked, but if I became a mother and anything happened to my baby because of my police work...I'd never be able to face life again." Michelle looked out of the rainy windshield. "Momma Peach, I...can I make a confession to you?"

"Yes, you can always confess your heart to me."

Michelle steadied her troubled mind. "I want to...marry Able. I know we belong together, Momma Peach. I haven't told him about Sung because...his life would be in danger. I'm worried that Able might...leave me...after he finds out the truth." Michelle sighed. "I know Able would catch the first flight to Georgia and come rushing to my rescue if he found out about Sung...I can't allow that." Michelle looked at Momma Peach. "I'm in love with Able and I know he's in love with me...but...having a family and being a cop...it doesn't match up. One or the other has to take a backseat, Momma Peach."

Momma Peach patted Michelle's hand. "I don't think Able will be mad at you for trying to protect him. But the time is going to come, when you're going to have to let

Able jump into the frying pan with you and sizzle some. A man like Able isn't afraid to stand by his woman and you're his woman. That man loves you in a way that is very—and I mean very—special. The way he looks into your eyes...oh baby, you're his entire world. Able would die for you in a split second if he had to. Why? Because, you're so very special. You're as beautiful as the softest summer night and as amazing as the birth of a new day. And don't get me started in on your heart." Momma Peach smiled and pushed Michelle's bangs away from her eyes. "Let's focus on tonight, and let tomorrow handle itself. And always know the Good Lord is in control of everything so whatever happens, well, will happen regardless of how much we try and stop it."

Michelle rubbed her cheek against Momma Peach's hand. Momma Peach was her momma—and she needed a momma. "Okay," she said and forced a brave smile to her face, "let's go see what's happening at the circus."

Michelle drove away from the curb and continued down the wet, dark streets. When she arrived at the fairgrounds, she saw Officer Chert's patrol car parked at the back of the parking field sitting deserted and bruised. Michelle drove up to the patrol car, retrieved her gun, and eased out into the rain with Momma Peach at her side. "Trunk is open," she said as her eyes walked around the darkness. Surely Lindsey was watching.

Momma Peach maneuvered her short little legs over to

the open trunk. The trunk was dark and empty, with a scattering of fishing gear, an empty rifle, a protective vest and some empty soda cans. "Well," she said, "one thing is for sure."

"What's that?" Michelle asked, running her hand over the empty rifle.

"Fred likes to fish," Momma Peach said and walked over to the driver's side door and poked her head into the car. A note was sitting in the front seat. "We have a note."

Michelle ran to Momma Peach. "What does it say?"

Momma Peach turned on the inside light and read the note: "Send the woman to Moroz's trailer and Michelle alone to the big tent with Hayman."

Michelle turned and looked at the dark circus. Not a single light was on in any of the trailers. The main tent sat like a dripping shadow, waiting to devour any person brave enough to step foot inside its mouth. "I guess this is where we part ways, Momma Peach."

Momma Peach didn't want to part ways. No sir and no ma'am. But what could she do to keep Michelle at her side? She felt her heart break. "You go handle that black widow...and I will go handle that crazy old Russian." Momma Peach grabbed Michelle's neck and hugged her. "Come back to me, Michelle. Do you hear me?"

"I will," Michelle promised and patted Momma Peach's

waist. "The gun hidden under your jacket fires easy, Momma Peach."

"I hate guns. I'll find a way to take down that old man without firing a shot," Momma Peach replied and looked into Michelle's eyes. "Baby, when you fight tonight, don't fight for anyone except your unborn child. Let that sweet future child be your strength, do you hear me? Fight for all the tomorrows you're going to have as a momma! Fight for all the diaper changes and first words and first steps...fight for your unborn child that you and Able will hold in your arms someday, do you hear me?"

Michelle felt a wonderful power enter her heart. "I never thought about it like that before, Momma Peach."

"Fight that awful woman as if she is holding your child captive and not a donut-bellied cop." Momma Peach spun Michelle around and patted her tush. "Go get her."

Michelle nodded and jogged off into the rain. As she did, Momma Peach broke down in tears. "And Lord, let her come back to me in one piece because I sure need her." With those words, Momma Peach began walking through the rain toward Max Moroz's trailer.

CHAPTER EIGHT

*M*ax Moroz was waiting for Momma Peach. "Hello there," he said in a calm voice as Momma Peach entered his trailer. His Russian accent purred a little, and the air in the room seemed colder to her. She shivered.

Momma Peach saw that Max was dressed in his clown costume. She could deal with that. What she couldn't deal with was the hideous, exaggerated clown makeup painted over his face. The makeup was done in black and white—an awful, tormented grin painted over his cheeks and lips. Large, deathless eyes peered out above a skeletal nose, eyes that were hungry for innocent victims. It was meant to be whimsical, but in the dark, rainy atmosphere, it looked like the designs of an insane, tortured child.

"You look as creepy as anything I have ever seen, old man," Momma Peach admitted, forcing her voice to remain calm. "But I know you under that paint, by your voice."

Max grinned and slowly showed Momma Peach the gun in his left hand and the kitchen knife he was holding in his right hand. Max's hands were covered over with black satin gloves with pom-poms around the cuffs, but the effect was sinister and cruel against the weapons. "Shut the door, lady," he ordered Momma Peach.

Momma Peach slowly closed the trailer door. One wrong move and Max would surely bypass the knife and shoot her dead. "What are you planning to do, old man?"

"Kill you, of course," Max promised Momma Peach in a sickly calm voice.

"Just like you killed Lance Potter?"

Max stared at Momma Peach. He was now completely in character. In his memory, he saw hard hands striking him, the frozen ground beneath his feet, the empty chill of a ravenous stomach denied day after painful day. Each painful memory empowered him—the clown would punish the adults and save the children. He felt his insanity ringing in his ears. "Lance Potter threatened my reputation. The man had to die."

"You're one sick puppy, old man," Momma Peach told Max. "You killed a good man just because he was a better clown than you?"

"No man is a better clown than Max Moroz," Max snapped at Momma Peach. He brandished the kitchen knife at her. "Ms. Sung paid me a recent visit, lady. It seems she is in a hurry to do away with you. I was intending to play with you a bit before ending your life. However, I have been ordered to skip my pleasure."

Momma Peach glanced around the trailer. She spotted certain items that she could use as a weapon if needed. But her main concern was to keep Max talking for the time being. She needed all the confession the man was willing to give to be picked up by the wire she wore under her jacket. "You know, at first I thought you were kinda decent. But then I saw your eyes and knew better. I wonder if Lance Potter, rest his poor soul, saw what I see in your eyes."

Max lowered the kitchen knife. He stared at Momma Peach with soulless eyes. "Lance kept his distance from me. Oh, he pretended to like me in front of the others, but his eyes spoke the truth. Lance knew my heart, lady."

"Seems like he knew a crazy old man when he saw one," Momma Peach told Max. "Tell me something since you're going to kill me, okay?"

Max stood silent and still, staring at Momma Peach through eyes that were no longer his own. "What?" he finally spoke.

"How did you kill poor Mr. Potter?"

Max grinned. "Very easily," he replied through a rotten mouth. "It was a foggy night here on the grounds." Max walked his mind back in time. "The fog was especially thick. I knew the fog would provide the perfect cover for my purpose." Max stared at Momma Peach, seeing only his own madness. "Shortly after midnight, I slipped out into the fog, dressed in the same way you see me now. I walked over to Lance's trailer and knocked on his door. When Lance answered, I simply asked if I could come in and explained that I thought I was having a mental breakdown and needed help. I was very clever."

"And poor Mr. Potter fell for your trap?" Momma Peach asked, listening to the heavy rainfall outside and wondering how Michelle was doing in the main tent.

Max nodded. "Yes. You see, weeks before I killed Lance I began letting on that I wasn't feeling well...mentally. I even admitted to him that I believed I was suffering a form of mental illness." Max continued to stare at Momma Peach. "When I arrived at Lance's trailer and asked for help, the man was more than willing to accommodate me, because even though he saw darkness in my eyes, he was still a bleeding heart." Max took a step toward Momma Peach. If the woman tried to run, he would shoot her. If he got close enough to attack, he would stab her. "When I entered Lance's trailer, I dropped to my knees and grabbed my chest and began begging for water."

"You sicko," Momma Peach said. "If I had my pocketbook with me I would beat you senseless."

Max ignored Momma Peach's comment. "When Lance walked past me I stood up behind him and..." Max grinned, "pulled my knife out and carried out the final act."

"Oh, don't make me smack that paint off your face!" Momma Peach yelled at Max in disgust.

Max lifted the kitchen knife in his hand. "The gun with your fingerprints on it," he told Momma Peach. "Ms. Sung now has that gun. She is going to kill your cop friend and place the blame on you. My job is to kill you and leave a suicide note beside your body claiming that you killed your cop friend because you thought she was Ms. Sung."

Momma Peach nodded and sucked her teeth, tasting the chili again. Mr. Sam and his cayenne pepper, she fussed in her mind. "So you two have it all figured out, huh? What about Mr. Hayman?"

Max stood very still. "Ms. Sung didn't mention Mr. Hayman to me."

Momma Peach nodded again. "Well, old man, you killed an innocent man and you're going to have to pay for your actions. I sure am going to be the one to make you pay, too."

"Max Moroz regretted killing Lance, but the clown did not," Max told Momma Peach with a little bow. "The clown always wins when he performs, lady. The clown is always hungry for revenge."

"Oh, give the horror stories a rest, will you?" Momma Peach asked. "Old man, you may look spooky, but underneath your costume and paint you're nothing but a worn-down, mentally deranged old man still whining about his childhood. I have news for you, boy...grow up! Ain't nobody in the world ever had the perfect childhood. Kids today whine and fuss when they have to make a bed but in the old days I scrubbed my momma's floors, yes sir and yes ma'am, because my momma liked a clean house."

Max took a step closer to Momma Peach. "Max Moroz isn't interested in your mother, and neither is the clown. Now be still, lady, because the clown is hungry." With those words, Max lunged at Momma Peach.

"Oh, goodness gracious alive, here we go, here we go!" Momma Peach yelled and backed up to a folding chair, grabbed it, and threw it at Max. The chair struck Max, knocked the gun out of his hand, and forced him back. "Stay back, old man," Momma Peach ordered and snatched up a juggling pin from a box on the table, dropped into a batter's position, and began swinging the bowling pin in the air. "I will knock your head clear to the moon, boy!"

Max looked down at the floor, spotted the gun, and then

looked back at Momma Peach. His eyes turned red with rage. "You will die, lady," he growled and lifted the kitchen knife into the air and took a swing at Momma Peach. Momma Peach swung the bowling pin at him, forcing Max to take a step back.

"I'll knock you clear into yesterday!" Momma Peach warned Max. "I don't take no nonsense off of folks, especially a fruitcake like yourself. You want a piece of me, come and get some, yes sir and yes ma'am!"

Max hissed. He was now determined to kill Momma Peach with his knife and ignored the gun on the ground. He stepped forward and swung the knife at Momma Peach. Momma Peach moved back and swung the bowling pin at the knife and almost hit it. Max stepped forward again and swung the knife even harder, coming mere inches from Momma Peach's face. But Momma Peach was fast. She ducked out of the way, bent low, and then came up swinging with the bowling pin the way a boxer would when aiming a vicious uppercut. The bowling pin struck the knife this time and knocked it out of Max's hand. Max stumbled backward, tripped over his feet, and crashed down to the floor. But he wasn't out. He quickly reached onto a nearby table, picked up a plastic squirt bottle of bathroom cleaner, and sprayed the bleach mixture at Momma Peach's face. Momma Peach quickly covered her face with her right arm and moved back to the end of the trailer. She bumped into a wooden chest, lost her balance, and plopped down.

Max crawled to his feet, gathered up his knife, and advanced on Momma Peach, spraying the hot water and bleach at her as he did, forcing her to cover her face. "Time to die!" he hissed and raised the knife in the air, preparing to carry out one final act.

"Not this time," Momma Peach yelled. She leaned back as fast as her body would let her, lifted her short little legs, and kicked both feet at Max just as Max lunged at her with his knife, prepared to strike. Momma Peach's feet caught Max in his chest. Max stumbled backward in the trailer, struggling to keep his balance, and finally came to a stop at his couch. Momma Peach jumped to her feet and pointed the bowling pin at him. "Come and get some, boy! I'm ready for round two, yes sir and yes ma'am!"

Max hissed. He had dropped the plastic bottle and Momma Peach had tossed it far behind the trunk where it was impossible to retrieve. There were no more ready weapons. The woman was becoming very problematic. Lance had been very simple to kill. He assumed Momma Peach would be easier than Lance. Instead, the woman was putting up a good fight. "You're going to die, lady. Why resist?" he asked and began walking toward Momma Peach.

Momma Peach prepared for round two. As soon as Max was close enough, he began swinging his knife at her face. Momma Peach ducked out of the way, wrapped her hands around the bowling pin as tight as she could, and swung at Max's knife hand with all of her strength. "Take this, you used-up toilet paper roll!" she yelled.

The bowling pin made contact with Max's hand. He yelled out in pain as the knife went crashing down to the floor. As soon as the knife hit the floor, Momma Peach dropped the bowling pin and charged at Max with a flying dive. All Max saw was Momma Peach flying through the air at him like an acrobat. Then he was on the floor with Momma Peach crushing his chest. He struggled to fight, but his old body finally gave out. With his last bit of strength, he thrust his right arm out for his knife, his hand shaking violently. But the clown failed to achieve its mission and Max's hand fell down onto the floor. Or so it seemed to Momma Peach. "Sick old skunk," she said and slowly began to crawl off of Max. As soon as she did, Max opened his eyes, a hideous monster coming back to life, grabbed his knife, and tried to stab Momma Peach in the back. The knife struck a protective vest.

"What?" Max wheezed as he tried to push the knife through the vest.

Momma Peach spun around and kicked the knife out of Max's hand. Max tried to stand up. "Oh stay down!" Momma Peach yelled and belly-flopped right on top of Max. The last thing Max remembered before falling unconscious was Momma Peach squeezing the air out of him. At last his head went limp and he did not move.

"Good grief," Momma Peach fussed to herself, "crazy old coot really stabbed me. Good thing Michelle forced me to wear this here vest." Momma Peach rubbed a spot between her shoulder blades and felt a tear in her jacket. "See what you did, old man? Now I'm going to have to do some sewing and I ain't especially fond of sewing." Momma Peach rolled her eyes. "If it ain't one crazy skunk trying to stink up my life it's another. What I need is a vacation to the middle a deserted island, but with my luck, I'd probably run into an angry cannibal. Oh, give me strength, give me strength."

Momma Peach quickly searched the trailer for some rope, located some in the wooden chest, and tied Max up tightly. "Stay put, old man," she said and hurried back out into the rain and got her short legs moving toward the main tent. But then she stopped, turned around and looked at Lionel's trailer. "Of course," she said. "Baby, hold tight and let me find Officer Chert."

Momma Peach turned and ran toward Lionel's trailer and found the front door unlocked. She yanked open the front door, rushed inside, and saw Fred Chert lying face down on the floor with his hands handcuffed behind his back and his ankles tied together. "Fred?"

"Momma Peach?" Fred asked, turning his head. "What in the world are you doing here? Where is Detective Chan?"

"No time to explain," Momma Peach said and squatted down next to Fred. "Where are your keys?"

"That woman took the keys to my handcuffs along with my gun," Fred Chert told Momma Peach in a voice filled with shame. "I sure let her fool me, Momma Peach."

Momma Peach patted Fred's back. "Baby, you're a man and ain't a man alive immune to a pretty face. Now let me think, okay?" Momma Peach stood up and searched the inside of Lionel's trailer. "Ain't nothing in here I can use," she said in a worried voice. "Fred, I'm going to untie them ropes around your ankles and then you're going to have to hightail it out of here with your hands handcuffed behind your back, okay?"

Fred nodded. What other choice did he have? "Okay, Momma Peach, but tell me one thing. Where is Detective Chan? That crazy woman who brought me is out to kill her."

"I know. I know," Momma Peach said and looked out of the front door toward the main tent.

Michelle stood before Lindsey Sung in the middle of the main tent. "Here I am, Sung," she said as the smell of hay and damp earth floated up into her nose.

Lindsey kept her hands behind her back. She was wet,

angry and feeling fatigue catching up to her. The fight would have to be quick and deadly. "Where is Mr. Hayman?" she demanded.

"He'll arrive soon enough," Michelle informed Lindsey. "One of my officers is bringing him here. A female officer. If you defeat me, you'll have no problem taking her out and getting to Hayman." Michelle took off her leather jacket and dropped it down to the ground. The tent was dark, but she could clearly make out Lindsey's figure with sharp eyes. "I gave direct orders to my people to stand down. Enough people have died, Sung. This fight ends with us. If you win, then Hayman is yours."

"If I win?" Lindsey laughed in a cynical voice. "Chan, do you really believe that you can defeat me? You're a foolish woman. I warned you to back off, didn't I? But did you listen? No. Now you must pay a heavy penalty for your ignorance." Lindsey laughed again. "Your little friend will, too. By now, I'm sure Moroz has ended her worthless life."

Michelle ignored Lindsey's hateful remark. "Where is Fred Chert?" she demanded.

"Alive," Lindsey said in a poisonous voice. "But he won't be after I've finished with you." Lindsey put on a pair of black gloves and pulled out a gun from under her leather jacket and aimed it at Michelle. "I could kill you right now, Chan."

Michelle remained calm. "You won't, though. Sung, guns are not your style. You're a fighter, like me. We were trained to battle with our bodies, not weapons."

Lindsey grinned. "Perhaps," she said and tossed the gun to the side. "That gun has your friend's fingerprints on it. She is going to be blamed for your murder after I make it appear that she committed suicide, of course." Lindsey removed her leather jacket and tossed it down onto the ground and dropped into a lethal fighting position. "Are you ready to die, Chan?"

Michelle prepared herself for battle. "As they say here in the deep south: Come and get some."

"Oh, I will," Lindsey promised and lunged at the approaching Michelle with a furious front kick. Michelle blocked the kick with her left arm, swung around, and smacked Lindsey in the face with her right fist. Lindsey stumbled backward, felt her face and then charged forward with a flurry of front kicks. Michelle stepped backward, blocking one kick after another. But then Lindsey changed her angle of attack and surprised her with a sudden roundhouse kick. The kick caught Michelle in the face and threw her down onto the ground. Michelle was not daunted, but in that split second, she scolded herself for not anticipating the ferocity of Lindsey's attacks.

Lindsey ran at Michelle, but Michelle flipped up off the ground, dropped down into a deep squat, and punched

Lindsey in the stomach. Lindsey doubled over, grabbing her stomach, and then recovered and charged forward again. Michelle shot up into the air, executed a vicious roundhouse kick, and caught Lindsey square in the face. Lindsey's body went twirling in the air and crashed down onto the ground. Michelle backed up a few steps and waited.

"You're good, but not good enough," Lindsey hissed as she flipped up to her feet and slowly began circling Michelle. She appeared only slightly winded from her exertions.

Michelle remained calm. In her mind, she saw a sweet, innocent baby cradled in her arms, smiling up at her with toothless gums, smelling of fresh baby powder, wrapped in a warm blanket. "For you," she promised.

"Die," Lindsey said and ran at Michelle and began kicking, throwing a series of front kicks, roundhouse kicks and leg sweeps at her. Michelle managed to block every kick but was finally caught with a painful leg sweep that knocked her down onto the ground. Lindsey came at her and began kicking at her face. Michelle caught Lindsey's right foot and pushed her backward, flipped up to her feet, but was brought down again by a powerful spin kick. Michelle felt her body launch through the air and hit the ground. Knowing that Lindsey would be on her in a matter of seconds, she shook off her pain and began rolling to her right side just as Lindsey began kicking at her face again. Michelle kept rolling, forcing Lindsey to chase her. Then she suddenly stopped, spun her body around in a flash, and managed to kick Lindsey's right leg hard enough to push the woman back. The fight had turned again.

As Lindsey stumbled back, Michelle jumped to her feet and crouched down. Lindsey ran at her with a flying kick. Michelle ducked the kick and used the opening to land a spin punch on Lindsey's face. Lindsey ignored her pain and kicked Michelle in her stomach and then charged at her. Michelle grabbed Lindsey by her shirt, then dropped onto her back, using the momentum to flip Lindsey over and into the air. Lindsey twirled in the air and managed to land on her feet. "Is that all you got, cop?" she asked, wiping her nose on her sleeve with a smirk.

Michelle jumped to her feet and steadied her fighting position. "I've got more, Sung," she promised.

Lindsey narrowed her eyes. Michelle was an experienced and skilled fighter; better than she thought. She was throwing everything she had at the woman and finding no clear victory in return. Lindsey steadied her mind and determined to wear Michelle down a little at a time, beginning with her arms. If she couldn't win on technique, she could certainly win on stamina. She drew in a deep breath and thrust her body forward and began punching and thrusting deadly pointed blows, kicking at

Michelle's arms, forcing Michelle to block each one, wearing down her muscles.

Michelle realized Lindsey's tactic, blocked a kick, and in the split second before Lindsey could throw the next punch, Michelle dropped down into a deep crouch and levered a powerful kick into the bone of her upper thigh. The blow was powerful enough to stop Lindsey momentarily, and she even stumbled backward. Michelle used the moment to back up and gain some more space. She had to keep that sweet future child in her mind, lest she be consumed with fear and what-ifs. She dropped into her fighting stance again.

The pain was incredible, but Lindsey didn't let on. Instead, she charged at Michelle again, determined to wear the woman's arms down. Michelle was quick with her hands but slower with her kicks. "Die!"

Michelle began blocking Lindsey's kicks again, feeling her arms growing tired. She started to realize that Lindsey was lethal with her kicks—more lethal than she was. Michelle knew her power was in her hands more than her legs. If Lindsey wore down her arms, she would be finished. "Not yet," Michelle said and began throwing her body backwards into a series of quick backflips, managing to put a little more distance between herself and Lindsey. Lindsey chased after Michelle, certain she could catch her prey, but ran into a hard spin punch when Michelle suddenly stopped her flips. The punch sent pain crashing through Lindsey's head and nearly caused her to black out. "Not bad, cop," she hissed unsteadily and backed away from Michelle a few feet in order to clear her mind.

Michelle felt exhaustion begin taking its toll. Her stomach was full of Sam's chili, too much coffee, and a candy bar she really didn't need. She was sure Lindsey's stomach only held water and maybe a simple veggie sandwich. She took in a deep breath and watched Lindsey begin circling her again and promised to sleep for an entire week and go on a healthy diet if she survived the fight. She held the snugly wrapped child in her arms, mentally telling Able and herself that she wouldn't lose sight of the goal. Before she could finish her thought, Lindsey charged forward with her front kicks again, forcing Michelle backward.

Lindsey knew Michelle was growing weaker and wouldn't be able to keep up her back flips all night. Michelle began blocking the kicks and tried to drop down into a defensive split again. As she did, Lindsey kicked her right in the face with a deadly front kick. Michelle felt her body fly backward and her world turned dark for a few seconds. Then she felt Lindsey kick her in the chest, forcing out all of the air in her lungs. Lindsey went for a second kick. This time Michelle managed to catch her foot and push her backward. Lindsey quickly caught her balance and charged forward again, kicking at Michelle, forcing her to roll from side to side, wearing out her body. Then, out of nowhere, she heard someone scream: "Incoming!"

Lindsey turned around and saw Momma Peach charging at her like a raging bull. Before she could react, Momma Peach headbutted her right in the stomach. Lindsey never felt such power. All she felt was her body fly back through the air and hit a wooden tent pole. "I'm here!" Momma Peach yelled and ran over to Michelle and helped her stand up.

"Whew, thanks, Momma Peach," Michelle said in grateful voice. "I wasn't doing so good."

Lindsey crawled to her feet, ran at Momma Peach, and threw a hard kick at her. "Die!"

"Oh no, you don't," Momma Peach yelled and swung her bowling pin as hard as she could into Lindsey's shin. Lindsey cried out in pain and stepped backward.

"You coward!" she yelled at Michelle, limping. "You're going to let that woman fight for you?"

Michelle looked at Momma Peach. "Think of your future child," Momma Peach reminded Michelle.

"I did," Michelle said in a worried voice. "Momma Peach, Lindsey is fast with her kicks. She is wearing me down."

Lindsey heard Michelle confess her weakness and grinned. Surely, she knew, if Momma Peach had not interfered in the fight, she would have finished Michelle off. "This is between you and me, Chan. Unless you're too much of a coward?"

Michelle stared at Lindsey. She wasn't a coward, and she was definitely prepared to die proving she wasn't a coward. "Calm down and remember your training in the old country," Michelle whispered. She felt Momma Peach touch her shoulder. "I can do this, Momma Peach. I can defeat Lindsey."

Momma Peach leaned forward and kissed Michelle on her cheek. "I'm right with you. Let's get her."

"No," Michelle told Momma Peach, "this is my fight." Michelle pulled Momma Peach behind her and dropped down into a fighting position. "Fight, Sung!"

Lindsey charged at Michelle and once again began throwing one powerful front kick at her after another. This time, Michelle was prepared. Instead of blocking the front kicks with her arms, she began blocking them with her defensive kicks. This caught Lindsey off guard and forced her to attempt a spin kick to get above Michelle's legs. Michelle ducked under the spin kick and brought both of her fists up into Lindsey's chest. Lindsey flew backward, rubbed her chest, and then charged forward again. Michelle ran at Lindsey and threw a kick at her. Lindsey easily avoided it but when she spun around to counter-attack, she was met by a lightning-fast punch...and then another punch...and another.

Michelle began throwing punches at Lindsey so fast that Lindsey finally turned and tried to run away from Michelle. Michelle threw her body forward and kicked Lindsey in the back. Lindsey toppled down to the ground, rolled off into the distance, and crawled to her feet. She saw Michelle's shadowy body standing very still, waiting for her. For the first time in her life, she felt fear enter her heart. Michelle wasn't a fighter...the woman was a warrior. Even if Momma Peach hadn't shown up, Lindsey knew that somehow Michelle would have managed to survive the fight. But even though fear entered her heart, she wasn't about to back down. She, too, was a warrior. "Die!" she yelled hoarsely and ran at Michelle and once more began throwing front kicks, determined to wear Michelle's arms down.

Michelle began blocking the front kicks with her own set of defensive kicks again, slowly backing away from Lindsey, trying desperately to think of an offensive attack that would catch her opponent off guard. But before she could, one of Lindsey's front kicks slipped past her defenses and caught her in the chest. Michelle felt her body fall backward and immediately tucked into a roll and popped up onto her feet, only to be met by a hard spin punch, followed by a painful kick to her right rib cage and then a leg sweep. Michelle felt her body crash down onto the ground but managed to catch Lindsey's right foot before it struck her feet. She threw Lindsey backward and jumped up to her feet. Lindsey ran at her and once again began throwing front kicks at her. Michelle became fed up with the front kicks, threw caution to the wind, and threw her body into a screaming roundhouse kick. She felt her right foot connect with Lindsey's face and throw the woman into the air. Lindsey flopped down onto the ground, shook her head, looked up at Michelle, and began crawling to her feet, slower than before. "Come get some, Sung!" Michelle yelled, feeling completely drained of energy. But in her mind, she kept seeing an innocent baby cradled in an achingly soft blanket, smiling at her with toothless gums.

"Knock her into the next century, baby!" Momma Peach yelled.

Lindsey shook her head. The roundhouse kick had really hurt her. She had never been kicked so hard in all of her life. Her vision was now blurry, and her mind fought to stay awake. She looked at Momma Peach and then back at Michelle. "I will not be a coward," she whispered and ran at Michelle. This time she didn't throw a single front kick. Instead, she grabbed the front of Michelle's shirt and began grappling with her. Michelle tried to stand strong, but Lindsey managed to trip her back legs and take her down onto the ground. Once on the ground, she began to wear out Michelle's arms by pinning her down, forcing her to block punches and elbow blows. Michelle struggled to block Lindsey's attacks and wrapped her legs around the woman's waist while using her arms to protect her face. "Time to die, cop!"

Michelle wasn't sure how much longer she could hold on. Lindsey had the upper hand, literally. All she could do was remain in a defensive position until she could figure out a way to throw Lindsey off her. But then, all of a sudden, Lindsey stopped punching at her and swayed for a moment. Before Michelle could process what she was seeing, Lindsey yanked a dagger out of a knife holster attached to her ankle, raised the dagger into the air, and prepared to stab Michelle in the chest. "Die!" Lindsey screamed and lunged at Michelle, the dagger high above her head. As she did, Momma Peach whacked her upside the head with her bowling pin. Lindsey caved, a stringless marionette, and dropped down onto the ground silent and unconscious. "If she doesn't play fair, then neither will I," Momma Peach told Michelle.

Michelle closed her eyes and drew in a few deep breaths. "Momma Peach, we need a vacation," she said and let her arms lay on the ground without moving them.

"Yes, we—" Momma Peach was interrupted by a bright flashlight beam. She looked over to her right and saw two men holding automatic machine guns. "Oh boy," she whispered and prepared for the worst while hoping being shot to death wouldn't be very painful.

CHAPTER NINE

*C*harlie Jones stepped between the two thugs holding the automatic rifles and aimed the flashlight in his hand at Michelle. "Detective Chan, I presume?" he asked in a thick Chinese accent.

"Yes," Michelle said and covered her eyes with her right hand and quickly stood up, ignoring her injuries.

"My name is Charlie Jones, Detective Chan," Charlie said in a very displeased voice. He looked at Lindsey Sung who lay unconscious on the damp ground. "I have come to end the troubles you have caused and retrieve my injured sister."

Momma Peach eased closer to Michelle. She studied Charlie with worried eyes. The man was of medium height, very thin, but with the face of a diseased tiger. The black suit he wore reminded her of Max Moroz's clown costume. Every deadly creature wore different costumes, but their motives were all the same. "Your sister is taking a nap, boy," she told Charlie.

Michelle eyed the two thugs standing next to Charlie. The thugs were mean in appearance, cold in the face, and programmed to kill when ordered. "Your sister is out of commission for now."

"I watched the fight," Charlie informed Michelle. "You did well against my sister. I should be impressed but I'm not. You have caused a considerable amount of trouble," Charlie told Michelle in anger. "Detective Chan, I want you to go get Lionel Hayman and bring him to me. If you do, I will take him and my sister and leave in peace. If you refuse," Charlie pointed at Momma Peach, "the woman dies."

Michelle looked at Momma Peach just as the sound of an approaching car filled her ears. "That's Joan with Mr. Hayman," she said loud enough for Charlie to hear.

Charlie looked toward the front of the main tent. "Who?" he demanded.

"Joan is one of my officers," Michelle explained. "I ordered her to bring Mr. Hayman to the circus thirty minutes after me. She's a little late, but better late than never."

Charlie nudged his two men. "Stand right where you are and wait," he told them and eased back. "I'll hide behind the bleachers just in case there's any funny business." Charlie jogged behind the bleachers and pulled out an ugly gun and waited. A few minutes later, he saw a woman cop walk into the main tent. A man with Lionel Hayman's distinct hair was walking beside the woman with his hands handcuffed in front of him. "Very good," Charlie whispered and began planning the death of Michelle, Momma Peach, Lionel and the woman cop.

"Here is Mr. Hayman," Millie spoke in a tough cop voice. She was wearing Joan's uniform and played the part perfectly.

Michelle glanced at Momma Peach.

"What's this about, then?" Sam fussed, keeping his head low and his face hidden. Sam's voice sounded identical to Lionel Hayman's; an English accent that was rich and plummy. How? Momma Peach wasn't sure, but she sure was excited to see her Mr. Sam.

"Shut up," Millie barked and shoved Sam forward. "Okay, Detective, here is your man." Millie pointed to the two thugs holding the automatic rifles. "Who are they?"

"Drop your gun, cop!" one of the thugs yelled and aimed his gun at Millie.

"Do as he says, Joan," Michelle said in a quick voice.

"I demand an explanation." Sam said.

Millie ordered Sam to shut up and threw the gun in her utility belt holster down onto the ground. She felt silly dressed as a cop—but hey, when a new adventure presented itself, you sure couldn't pass it by, now could you? "Okay, okay, take it easy, pal."

Momma Peach wanted to hug Sam and Millie but resisted. Her babies were sure hard-headed, but they had come to their rescue. Sometimes, she grinned, being a little hard-headed was a good thing, especially in Georgia. "Okay," Michelle called out, "Hayman is here."

Charlie began to step out from behind the bleachers. As he did, Old Joe appeared in the shadows and smacked the man right in the face with a wooden cane. Charlie saw stars and crashed backward. Old Joe, not one to waste any time, quickly slapped the gun out of Charlie's hand with his cane and then finished the man off with one more grand wallop to the face. Charlie Jones (or whoever the man was) landed face-first on the ground, out cold. Old Joe nodded even though he was scared half to death. "I think that's a home run Momma Peach, but you're gonna give Old Joe more gray hair than he needs," he whispered and then began tying Charlie up with some rope he had found.

"Charlie, get out here!" one of the thugs yelled, "Hayman is here."

Michelle waited for Charlie to appear. As she did Lindsey began coming to. Michelle knew if the woman came to, she would recognize the ruse with Sam's disguise and ruin the whole thing. She had to act. But how? The two thugs had their rifles aimed straight at Momma Peach. One wrong move and Momma Peach was a goner. Sam came to her rescue. He broke free of Millie and started walking toward the two thugs. "Get me out of here at once," he ordered them in his deeply British accent. "Mr. Wong will be hearing from me about this appalling treatment."

The two thugs froze. The mentioning of Mr. Wong's name sent chills through their minds. "Charlie, get out here!" one of the thugs called out again.

Sam reached into the side pocket of his jacket and pulled out the fax Old Joe had stolen—a fax Old Joe came across in his own pocket while pacing around Michelle's office worrying about Momma Peach and Michelle. The fax held the name to one of the most powerful men in China. "I want to speak to Mr. Wong right this minute," Sam demanded in an accent that fooled even Lindsey.

Lindsey managed to open her eyes. Her vision was blurry. All she saw through the darkness were two men holding rifles and a man who she thought was Lionel Hayman, walking toward them. But the man she saw was oddly a little taller than Lionel. "That's...not...him," she whispered, unable to carry her voice out into the open air.

"I demand to speak to Mr. Wong!" Sam fussed.

The two thugs looked at each other with worried eyes. "Charlie, get out here," they both yelled. "Hayman is here. We have the package."

Charlie lay silent as Old Joe tied him up. "Where is he?" one of the thugs asked his sidekick.

Michelle glanced over at Lindsey. The woman was struggling to lean up on her arms. If Lindsey managed to get up and regain her full power, she would kill everyone. "Momma Peach," Michelle whispered, "when I give you the signal, throw the bowling pin in your hand up in the air."

"Baby?" Momma Peach whispered back.

"Please, trust me," Michelle begged.

"I trust you," Momma Peach promised Michelle.

Sam stopped a few feet away from the two thugs, deliberately placing his body between them and Momma Peach. "Uncuff me at once!"

Michelle glanced at Millie. Millie eased closer to her and slipped a can of pepper spray from the utility belt into her hand while Sam occupied the two thugs. Michelle glanced at Lindsey again. Lindsey was gaining strength. "That's...not...Hayman!" Lindsey finally managed to call out.

"What?" the two thugs yelled.

"Kill him!" Lindsey screamed as she struggled to sit up.

Sam knew it was time to act. He broke his hands apart from the fake cuffs over his wrist and brought up a gun. "Drop your weapons!" he yelled and aimed the gun in his right hand at the thug standing in front of him. "Now!"

Instead of doing as ordered, both thugs began backing up. Michelle knew that Sam wouldn't shoot unless he was fired on and the two thugs were going to open fire at any second. Time was of the essence. "Now!" she yelled at Momma Peach.

"Okay!" Momma Peach tossed the bowling pin up into the air. Michelle launched her body up and kicked the bowling pin as hard as she could. The bowling pin went flying at the two thugs and struck one of them in the face, knocking the man out cold. The second thug, seeing that the other man was now disabled, began to fire on Sam. Sam dropped down onto one knee and squeezed off a single shot. A bullet erupted from the barrel of his gun and struck the second thug in his firing hand. The thug cried out in pain as the rifle in his hand went crashing down to the ground. "Not a move!" Sam yelled, "or the next one will be a kill shot, pal!"

The second thug nursed his wounded hand and stood very still. Lindsey hissed to herself, climbed to her feet, spotted the gun with Momma Peach's fingerprints on it lying close to her feet, and quickly scooped the gun up.

She aimed the gun straight at Momma Peach. "Drop your weapon or she dies!" she yelled at Sam.

Sam spun to his side and saw Lindsey aiming a gun at Momma Peach's chest. Lindsey Sung was too far away for him to attempt a clear shot without risking Momma Peach's life. He had no other choice but to drop his gun. "Okay, okay," he said and threw his gun down onto the ground. "Take it easy."

Lindsey growled. Her head felt bashed in and her mind fuzzy. Yet she was clear enough in her thinking to realize that she had to kill everyone in the tent, beginning with Momma Peach. "It's time to die," she told Momma Peach and stepped forward. "But first I want to know where Hayman is hidden!"

"Oh, go eat a rotten piece of okra you pathetic worm," Momma Peach fired at Lindsey. "Kill me if you want, but you ain't gonna get your grubby claws on Mr. Hayman. We hid him real good, gal. Mr. Hayman has agreed to work on the right side of the law in exchange for a deal."

Lindsey narrowed her eyes. So Hayman had decided to betray Mr. Wong. She wasn't surprised. She never did trust Lionel Hayman to begin with. Forcing the man to carry out a contract signed by his brother had been foolish. However, if she returned to Mr. Wong empty-handed, she would be killed. Lionel Hayman was her responsibility. "Mr. Jones, get out here!" Michelle yelled and rubbed the back of her head with her left hand. Her vision was still blurry. She was seeing two of Momma Peach. "Mr. Jones—"

"Your fella is out cold," Old Joe said, stepping out from behind the bleachers and, without saying another word, began firing Charlie Jones' gun at Lindsey.

Lindsey, shocked to see Old Joe instead of Charlie, dived down onto the ground and began rolling into the darkness. As she did, Michelle grabbed Momma Peach and Millie and ran them behind the bleachers as Sam retrieved his gun and searched for Lindsey. Lindsey managed to blend in with the dark shadows consuming the tent. "Get over here, Sam," Old Joe begged.

Sam hurried over to Old Joe. "You're something else," he told Old Joe. "I thought I told you to stay at the station."

Old Joe patted Sam's shoulder. "Family sticks together," he actually smiled.

Lindsey searched the darkness and spotted Sam and Old Joe. She fired off a single bullet. The bullet struck the bleachers. Sam grabbed Old Joe and pulled him down. "Die," Lindsey hissed and began crawling on her stomach like a snake, making her way toward the bleachers unseen and unheard.

"You guys," Michelle told Millie, "were supposed to stay in my office."

Millie hugged Michelle and then hugged Momma Peach. "We gals gotta stick together."

Momma Peach squeezed Millie like a mother bear hugging her lost child. "Oh, I love me a good friend, yes sir and yes ma'am, I love you, Millie!"

Millie felt an incredible love—the sweetest love she had ever felt—coming from Momma Peach right into her heart. She nearly began to cry. "I love you, too, Momma Peach. I love you both. Now," Millie smiled, "sit back and watch the grand finale."

"Grand finale?" Michelle asked.

"You'll see," Millie promised. "Sam...Old Joe?"

"Up here," Sam whispered.

Millie grabbed Momma Peach's hand and hurried her up to Sam. "Where is the woman?" she asked.

"Somewhere out there," Sam whispered. "Out there in that darkness."

Lindsey's eyes might have been failing her, but her ears were crystal clear. She heard Sam whispering, aimed her gun in his direction, and fired off a shot. The bullet missed Sam by a long shot but did cause the man to duck and cover. "Die," Lindsey hissed again and continued to crawl toward the bleachers and then stopped and focused on the two automatic rifles lying on the ground. The thug with the wounded hand was hunkered down, uncertain what to do. Lindsey grinned, jumped to her feet and ran over to one of the rifles and snatched it up. "Time to die, all of you!" she yelled and turned around, getting ready to spray the bleachers with a shower of bullets.

Sam saw Lindsey grab the automatic rifle and yelled: "Get down, she's going to cover us with bullets!"

Lindsey grinned. She would kill her enemies and, somehow, find Hayman and kill him. "No one defeats Lindsey Sung," she yelled and began to fire. As she did, a loud, thunderous scream erupted. The ground began to shake. Lindsey spun around and looked at the front entrance of the tent. There, charging into the tent, was Melanie the elephant with Lidia riding on top of her. As deadly and daring as Lindsey Sung was, elephants terrified her. She hated elephants and feared them. "No!" Lindsey screamed and began backing up, her dizziness making it hard to move quickly.

Melanie narrowed her eyes and let out a thunderous roar and charged at Lindsey. "No!" Lindsey screamed and tried to run. She spun around and did not see the unconscious thug lying on the ground and tried to run. She tripped over the inert body and crashed down onto the ground. "No...no....noooo!" Lindsey cried out and threw her hands over her face as Melanie trampled over her body...not just once, but many times.

"Get her girl!" Lidia yelled out in triumph. She knew that

even her gentle elephant would not let a bully harm their friends.

Millie smiled at Momma Peach and Michelle. "See, girls, we circus folk have things under control."

Sam wiped his brow. Old Joe let out a deep breath. Michelle bowed her head in relief. Momma Peach simply walked out from behind the bleachers, approached Melanie, and gave the elephant the biggest hug in the world.

"My sweet girl," Momma Peach whispered and then kissed Melanie on her trunk. "Oh, how I love you."

Outside, the rain continued to fall. The show would not go on this time, and nor would the killers and their circus.

Able tapped the edge of Michelle's desk with his right hand. "You should have let me know you were in danger," he fussed. "I would have—"

"I know you would have," Michelle told Able in a loving, worried voice. "Able, honey, I didn't want you to get hurt. I know I was wrong, and I promise to never keep you in the dark ever again. It's just that...Lindsey Sung was a very dangerous woman, honey."

Able stared into Michelle's beautiful face and thought about how much he loved her. Instead of remaining upset, he simply smiled. "I know you meant well and were only trying to protect me, but, please, I'd rather die at your side than live without you, okay?"

Michelle felt a tear slip from her eyes. There in front of her stood a man wearing the ugliest green shirt she had ever seen tucked into a pair of dorky brown pants, with his hair messy and the right side of his mouth smudged with chocolate, yet she loved the man more than she could say. "You have a bit of chocolate right there," Michelle told Able. She wiped her tear away and then walked over to Able and wiped the chocolate off his mouth.

Able smiled, gently kissed Michelle, and then pulled her into his arms. "You look very tired."

"I am," Michelle confessed. She felt old and exhausted in her black leather jacket. "Honey—"

Able reached out and touched Michelle's lip. "I talked with Momma Peach. She told me everything," he said. "I know what you're going to say, and the answer is no."

"No?" Michelle asked.

"Baby, you're a cop and a great cop at that." Able nudged Michelle's nose with his. "Someday, I pray, you and I will get married. When that day comes, I know we'll decide on having a family together."

"Which means my life as a cop will have to come to an end," Michelle told Able in a sad voice.

"No, it doesn't."

"Yes, it does, honey. I can't put the life of my husband and children in danger," Michelle explained. "Able, what if...what if we have a child and someone like Lindsey Sung harms our child?"

Able took Michelle's hands into his own. "Michelle, there are thousands of cops out there that have families. It's a risk, I know, but without them, where would this country be?" Able looked into Michelle's teary eyes. "You're a cop, and you always will be, and I'll stand by you forever, okay? Someday when we have a family, your family will stand by you."

Michelle didn't know what to say. All she could do was wrap her arms around Able and cry. Momma Peach smiled, nodded at Sam and Millie, and walked out into the hallway.

"Well," she said and popped a piece of peppermint into her mouth, "I'm going back to my bakery to make some of my famous peach pies, yes sir and yes ma'am, and let my girls have the day off."

Sam shoved his hands down into his pants pockets. "Are you still mad over my chili, Momma Peach?"

Momma Peach grinned. "Oh, I'm not mad, but I did go

buy a few cans of cayenne pepper for supper tonight. You're going to love my special meatloaf, Mr. Sam...I'm making it just for you. The rest of us are having some good old, down-home, barbeque chicken." Momma Peach tipped a wink at Millie and smiled. "Don't you look pretty in that blue dress, Miss Millie, but don't wear it to supper tonight because the sauce will be a-flyin'."

"Yes, Momma Peach," Millie smiled back and nudged Sam with her elbow. "You better bring some Pepto Bismol with you, Sam."

Sam groaned. "Yeah, I reckon I better," he agreed and then looked at Momma Peach. "So what's going to happen, Momma Peach?"

"Oh," Momma Peach said and chewed on her peppermint, "Lindsey Sung is now six feet under. That crazy old Russian clown died of a heart attack after they got him in custody. The FBI has come and fetched Lionel Hayman," Momma Peach explained, "and that kooky Mr. Jones, if that was his real name, and his two armed thugs are behind bars, and the circus, well, it's no longer on the road."

"What about Mr. Wong?" Millie asked in a worried voice. "A man like that won't take getting punched in the face lightly."

Momma Peach shrugged her shoulders. "Baby, we shut down one black market operation and rustled up a few bad guys, but a man like Mr. Wong will just open a new operation and hire more bad guys. It's a never-ending cycle. I don't think Mr. Wong will bother with our town anymore. Men like that don't like stepping in dog poo twice." Momma Peach looked at Michelle's office. "At least he better not. If he does, well, I am always ready to tangle. I got my bowling pins ready. Or juggling pins. Whatever them things are."

Sam stared at Momma Peach. "You're quite a woman, Momma Peach," he said and put his arm around her. "You are quite a woman."

"Don't you forget it either, Mr. Sam," Momma Peach smiled. "Now, you two better get back to the farm and check on my sweet Lidia and Melanie. Oh, and speaking of Melanie...I sure am glad you've decided to keep her full-time."

"Well, Melanie did save the day," Sam explained and walked Momma Peach out into a fresh, soft, cool morning filled with autumn leaves dancing in the air. Fall was approaching as summer was fading. The air smelled of pumpkins and apple spice. The small Georgia town surrounding the police station, even though it didn't possess all of autumn's qualities due to its southern location, hugged the approaching season with loving arms nonetheless. "Lidia has decided to stay on at the farm with Millie. We're going to build a second house on the north part of the land."

"That's right," Millie smiled. "Lidia and I are going to be neighbors."

"Until the wedding bells ring and then sweet Lidia might be living alone," Momma Peach winked at Millie and Sam. She drew in a deep breath of air and smiled with happy eyes. "I think I will walk to the bakery this morning. You two scoot on back to the farm and give Melanie a kiss from me."

Sam blushed. He liked Millie and he knew Millie liked him. But marriage? At his age? He looked at Millie. Millie nudged him with her arm, smiling. "Come on old man, let's go. See you tonight for supper, Momma Peach."

"You bet," Momma Peach said and watched Millie walk Sam over to his truck. After Sam pulled away, she began a cozy walk back to her bakery, humming along the way, walking down sleepy streets filled with the scent of autumn, which reminded her of football and pumpkin pie. She spotted a few kids riding their bikes, talking and just enjoying the early morning. The sight of the kids made her heart smile as she walked past warm homes filled with good folk. "Oh yes, amazing grace, how sweet the sound," Momma Peach began to sing to herself as she continued on toward her bakery.

When she reached the main street where her bakery was located, she paused. "What a sight for sore eyes," Momma Peach whispered, soaking in the sight of the street, the familiar buildings, the trees and the sidewalk tables. She saw early morning delivery trucks conducting their business and familiar friends arriving to open their stores. "Oh, how sweet the sound," she smiled and waved at all of her friends and walked down to her bakery. Old Joe was sitting outside at the cast iron table when she arrived. He greeted her, but he had a bothered expression on his face. "Good morning. Something bothering you, Old Joe?" Momma Peach asked.

"Oh, hey, Momma Peach," Old Joe said and slumped down in his chair.

"Oh, give me strength," Momma Peach begged, "Old Joe is upset. What's the matter with you, old man?" Momma Peach asked. She sat down across from Old Joe and waited for the old conman to answer her.

"Them girls," Old Joe tossed a thumb at the bakery. "Mandy and Rosa. First they lock me in that there cellar and then they treat me like I'm some kind of a hero. I can't figure them out, Momma Peach. Just last night they took me out to a fancy supper with all the trimmings. Today...well, it's my turn to open the bakery, but they're already both inside, doing my morning chores. I think they're just making fun of Old Joe."

Momma Peach grinned. "Well, Old Joe, you old skunk, it seems to me that you don't know how to handle being loved."

Old Joe looked at Momma Peach and rolled his eyes. "Love...ha," he huffed.

"Oh?" Momma Peach asked and widened her grin. "Maybe they just like to help you because they like you, you old coot."

Old Joe rolled his eyes again, but deep down, he didn't mind being loved. What bothered him was...well, he was wondering how to show love back. "I reckon those girls ain't too bad," he confessed. "I guess...well, I'm kinda taking a liking to them. They both call me Gramps now...and I reckon that's not too bad, either."

Momma Peach nodded. "They are two very special girls, Old Joe. They love from their hearts, so don't fight against it." Momma Peach reached across the table and patted Old Joe's hand. "You'll do," she smiled at him. "All of us, Old Joe, are very fond of you."

"An old conman like me?" Old Joe asked.

"You ain't an old conman no more," Momma Peach promised. "Old Joe, you showed a great deal of bravery the other night at the circus. You risked your life to help your friends. A conman wouldn't do that, now would he? No sir and no ma'am, he sure wouldn't."

"Oh, I was just worried, that's all."

"Sure you were, and that's called love," Momma Peach patted Old Joe's hand again. "I will sure tell you that Mr.

Sam thinks the world of you, and Michelle...well, just let anyone look at you the wrong way and she'll set them straight."

Old Joe smiled. "Who'd ever think a man like me would be fond of a cop? I reckon Michelle is special too, though."

"You reckon?" Momma Peach asked.

Old Joe looked up and down the cozy street. "Okay, okay, Michelle...that woman, dag blast it, has worked her way into my heart. But not a word to her, you hear, Momma Peach? I can't let a cop think she's won me over."

Momma Peach smiled into Old Joe's eyes. "You know, for an old skunk, you're not half bad...just as long as you don't try and weasel money out of anyone again."

Old Joe rolled his eyes. "Yeah, yeah," he said and stood up. "I think I will walk down to the diner and get a cup of coffee."

"Oh?" Momma Peach asked in a tone that caused Old Joe to flinch.

"If I can stand the mud the diner serves as coffee, that is," Old Joe said in a quick voice and began backing away from Momma Peach. "I'll be back and start sweeping the floors in a bit, Momma Peach," he promised and scooted away.

Momma Peach rolled her eyes. "Yeah, yeah, you old

skunk," she said and walked into her bakery. She found Mandy and Rosa at the front counter wearing similar autumn-hued dresses that made them appear soft and lovely. "Oh, my girls," Momma Peach said. She ran up to Mandy and Rosa and pulled them into her arms. "I have missed my babies so much."

Mandy and Rosa hugged Momma Peach back. They were sure glad to see her. "We've missed you even more, Momma Peach," they promised and kissed Momma Peach on her cheek.

Momma Peach felt tears begin falling from her eyes. "I ain't been around too much lately, but that's going to change," she promised and looked into Mandy and Rosa's beautiful faces. "My sweet babies."

Mandy and Rosa hugged Momma Peach again and then looked out of the new front display window. "Momma Peach, last night," Mandy said in a sad voice, "Rosa and I both had upsetting phone calls."

"Oh?" Momma Peach said and set her pocketbook down on the front counter.

"Our boyfriends broke up with us," Rosa sighed. "But we're okay, really. Mandy and I have decided to put on brave faces today and shine brightly in the bakery for every customer who walks in. That's why we wore these dresses."

Momma Peach nodded. "You two sweet girls were too good for those boys anyway," she said in a motherly voice.

"Still hurts," Mandy admitted.

"I know," Momma Peach said and hugged Mandy and Rosa again. "But," she added in a positive voice, "there are plenty of fish in the sea, babies and—" the sound of a buzzing fly caused Momma Peach to freeze. She looked toward her new display window and saw the fly. "Oh, you little critter," she growled.

Mandy grinned at Rosa, rolled up the morning newspaper, and handed it to Momma Peach. Momma Peach took the morning newspaper and began creeping over toward the display window that was filled with delicious pies. "There she goes," Mandy said and leaned against the front counter.

"Good to have Momma Peach back," Rosa beamed and watched Momma Peach inch closer to the fly. The fly lazily flew away before finding out what she brandished in her hand.

"I'll get you yet!" Momma Peach yelled and began swinging the newspaper at the fly like a wild woman. The fly buzzed around her head and then flew off to another part of the bakery. Momma Peach pointed at Mandy and Rosa. "Not a word, babies," she ordered. Mandy and Rosa held their hands up in the air and promised to be quiet. Momma Peach nodded and began a second attack on the fly, believing the fly would be her only problem, not knowing a dark storm was brewing on the horizon. "Come to Momma Peach, you rotten devil!" Momma Peach said and charged at the fly again.

"Well," Mandy whispered to Rosa, "it's good to have things back to normal for a change."

"Yep," Rosa agreed and watched Momma Peach swat a piece of a pie onto the floor. "I'll get the broom, you get the dustpan."

Outside, the soft and gentle morning continued to blossom into a beautiful day as the words, "I'll get you, you blasted fly!" floated up and down Main Street. All of Momma Peach's friends smiled. It was sure good having Momma Peach back at work and ready to bake some more of her famous peach pies. Of course, the fly probably didn't think so. No sir and no ma'am. Not at all.

ABOUT THE AUTHOR

Wendy Meadows is an emerging author of cozy mysteries. She lives in "The Granite State" with her husband, two sons, two cats and lovable Labradoodle.

When she isn't working on her stories she likes to tend to her flowers, relax with her pets and play video games with her family.

Get in Touch with Wendy
www.wendymeadows.com